THE WIZARD KILLER

- SEASON ONE -

BY

ADAM DREECE

ADZO Publishing Inc.
Calgary, Canada

ADZO Publishing Inc.
Calgary, Alberta, Canada
www.adzopublishing.com

Printed in Canada

This is a work of fiction. Names, characters, places, and incidents are a product of the author's imagination. Locales and public names are sometimes used for atmospheric purposes. Any resemblance to actual people, living or dead, or to businesses, companies, events, institutions, or locales is completely coincidental.

Library and Archives Canada Cataloguing in Publication

Dreece, Adam, 1972-, author
        The wizard killer (season #1) / Adam Dreece.

Issued in print and electronic formats.
ISBN 978-0-9948184-5-4 (paperback).--ISBN 978-0-9948184-6-1
(mobi)

        I. Title.

PS8607.R39W59 2016   C813'.6   C2016-902303-6
                                         C2016-902304-4

2 3 4 5 6 7 8 9 2016-07-22 28,451

DEDICATION

To my wife,
who has either become a firm believer in me as an
author, or has completely lost her marbles. Either way,
the journey's fun,

To my daughter,
who surprised me by loving this tale and asked me
when the next one would be ready,

And to my friend Evan,
whose amazing support and encouragement helped
me to keep going in those moments when I wasn't
sure.

my love of serials

A long, long time ago I used to write 1960s style bubble-gum super-hero serials with some friends. I was a HUGE comic book fan (I still have 1500 comics, bagged and boarded, in my basement). Writing episodes was a fun, mind-bending challenge. Each episode needed to be gripping on its own, but all of them together had to weave a coherent tale that looked like I'd written them all together. Some things never change.

When I was writing my first science fiction book, The Man of Cloud 9, I decided to give myself a ludicrous stretch goal. On top of writing that book, doing book signings, giving talks, taking care of my 3 kids, blogging, and so on, why not commit myself to writing and posting meaty episodes each and every week. Sure, not a problem. I don't need to sleep, right?

It was scary, posting raw works like that. I kept expecting to find an excuse why I would stop, but I didn't.

At first, I figured no one was going to read it, but boy was I wrong. The Wizard Killer had a wildly diverse group of fans. Some would run to my website within minutes of new episodes being posted, and wanted more, NOW!

So for 20 weeks, I brought readers along with me on an amazing and intense adventure. While sometimes I'd sketch on paper where things might go ahead of time, until I was happy with the words on the screen, I didn't know where things would really end up.

While this version's been tweaked and professionally edited, it's still very much exactly what we all went through, only you don't have to wait a week between episodes. So welcome to a very different side of me, the side of me that's the story-teller who stares at the camp-fire with a hot cup of tea in his hands, and spins you a tale.

- Adam

episode one

Raw, stabbing pain rouses me from my dreamless sleep. I try opening my eyes, but they protest. I compromise and stare out the thinnest of slits at the obnoxiously bright, summer day and its blue sky.

I know my heart's pounding furiously, though I can hardly feel anything. My thoughts are a jumbled mess, but one keeps rising to the top of the heap: use every second. I don't know why.

With a focusing breath, I realize I've got intense pain coming from my lower body somewhere. I attempt to get up, but can't. Something's holding me down. I force my head up and see the hilt of my short sword, sticking out of my abdomen, and pinning me.

Closing my eyes, I struggle to remember what happened. My memories feel like someone threw them all on the floor, threw some fake ones on top, and then stomped on them until nothing made sense anymore. I think I was seeking revenge, and was reckless. The heat of the emotions are still warm inside. I didn't care who knew what I was up to, or what type of mess I created for myself, as long as the person died. Who the yig was I trying to kill? Did they turn the tables on me or did someone else kill me? It doesn't matter. I'm thankful that whoever did me in used my short sword, otherwise I'd be dead-dead.

The sick feeling in the pit of my stomach tells me that the world's magic has failed again, but I know it won't last. No time to wonder how many opportunities I've missed to come back, I've got to take this one. My sword's suspend-life enchantment is going to kick back in, and then I'll be stuck here until either its mana runs out and I die, or… Stop thinking about it and get moving.

Dropping my head and gratefully allowing my eyes to close again, I fumble about with my numb hands until I find the simple hilt of the sword. I push up against the hilt of the sword with everything I've got, kicking with my legs until finally it breaks free of the ground's grip. It comes out of me and goes flying, clattering on stone somewhere.

Yig, the pain's intense. I put a hand on my abdomen, pressing as hard as I can to slow the bleeding. "Now all I need is for magic to come back…" A nervous chuckle escapes. "Come on… don't tell me I've been out long enough that magic fails for days now. I'm not interested in dying today, though I appreciate the scenery," I mutter, distracting myself.

Grimacing and groaning, I roll myself onto my side and crawl over to my short sword. Its common appearance has fooled many. "Waiting's always fun…" I say through gritted teeth. Scanning about, I confirm that I'm in the same forested mountain clearing where I was killed last time. Funny how history repeats itself. Breathing deeply to focus, I rest my head and mutter to myself, trying to stay awake. Every now and then, I try to remember anything about what happened or my past, but I can't get a single clear memory to come forward. "This didn't happen last time."

The pain kicks up another notch. "Gah! Mother of Mercy… Come on, is that the best you can do? I can take it." I wish desperately for something, some sound to keep me company, to engage with me.

Finally, I feel a twist in my stomach. Magic's back. I wearily pick up my short sword and lay it on my chest, surprised by how tremendously heavy it is. With a shallow breath, I fight against my eyes closing. "Not now, come on… cowards." I feel for the base of the blade and run my thumb along the etched markings. A wave of warmth rushes through my body, and I sigh as my wounds close, the pain drifts away, and energy rushes in. "Once again we go from nemesis to friend, don't we?" I say dropping the sword to my side.

Staring up at the sky, I laugh. "Are you listening right now, Old Man? You were right, twice now. *Bring the weapon of your own demise for your enemy will relish in using it*, you said." I sit up and scratch my heavily bearded face. "It's like you knew or something. Maybe having…" There's nothing there, no memory or instinct.

Shaking it off, I feel my head, surprised to find my hair comes down to my shoulders. Pulling it front of my eyes, I'm relieved to see that it's still black, mostly. I tap the sword on the flat boulder I've been laying on as a goodbye, and stand up. Scratching my thick, scruffy beard, I notice a piece of vine wrapped around my wrist. Touching it, it instantly disintegrates, almost making me doubt it was even there. I recall that it's one of the Old Man's tricks for keeping track of time, but the details escape me. "Does that mean days or weeks?"

The screech of a bird overhead gets my attention and reminds me to get on with it. I smile. This time, I'm not going to be reckless and go after revenge at any cost. This time, I'm not going to get caught.

episode two

Scratching the back of my neck, I figure I should get moving, though to where, I haven't a clue. I try to sheath my short sword and find that I have neither a belt loop nor scabbard. All I'm wearing is my bloody shirt, with a conspicuous hole, and a pair of plain, brown pants. My rough leather shoes are within an inch of useless.

I search the clearing, certain that I left a cache of supplies, decent clothing... maybe weapons? It feels like the type of thing I'd do, but there's nothing. Was I killed unexpectedly? I find that hard to believe. Same place as last time, and I left nothing. Who else would have known to come *here*, of all places?

Pacing about, I glance at my wrist and wonder. Maybe I've been dead long enough that someone just happened upon my stuff. Biting my lip, I decide best to give up and move on. No telling if anyone's going to come through here soon.

Walking over to a boulder, I climb up to get a good look around. The clearing area is smooth, glacially-scrubbed stone. As though there would be a storybook giant buried under it. A few determined plants are eking out an existence in the sparse soil, but life doesn't seem to really start until the edges, a hundred yards away. To the west begins the forest of leafy trees, and to the east is the mountain. To the north and south are just rocky plains.

I glance up at the sky, and give myself a mental push to head west. I suspect I won't have to traipse through the forest for long before I come to a road. Giddy joy breaks out on my leathery face. The thought of gritty, noisy civilization never seemed so wonderful.

About an hour or two down the road, something comes into view. Not feeling particularly brazen, I decide to move along the tree line rather than stay on the road. Though the trees aren't packed in tightly, some cover is better than none at all.

As I approach carefully from the sides, I see it's a charred carriage of some kind. On its back is a metal tank that's partially intact. Closing my eyes for a second, I nod as something breaks through the inner fog. "Levi-cars... right." I'd forgotten about the levitating carriages and other luxuries of life. What I wouldn't give for a working one now.

Scanning about first, I approach to investigate. Clearly there had been bandits or some form of attack once upon a time. Given the look of the levi, it looks like it happened a while ago.

It's an elongated levi-car, its chassis entirely made of metal. It looks like something punched right through the roof, and a quick examination shows the insides are charred. Whatever decorated the interior is burned, fused or melted. It's like some wizard or acolyte managed to set off a fireball from within it. That would have taken some serious skill, not to mention a brazen disregard for self-preservation. I can't see any signs of bodies or remains, though it's possible they're part of what's fused to the metal.

Rubbing my hand along the inside, I can still sense mana residue, which confounds me. This can't be that old, then. Maybe a few weeks at most.

Curious, I put my blade down and give the metal carcass a shove. Double checking that I don't have any unexpected admirers, I give the carriage a more serious push. It moans but doesn't roll. Refusing to give in, I put everything I've got into it and laugh as it finally tips over in a puff of road dust. There is a classic panic-box underneath. It seems that someone else is just as paranoid as I am when they travel.

The lock gives way with a sharp hit from the end of my sword. "Hello my beauty," I say, carefully lifting a sleek pistol out and marveling at it. A dark blue engraved line runs along the edge of its long barrel to the end of the handle. It fits like a glove in my hand. I point it at a tree, staring down its barrel, appreciating the perfect weight. The design looks familiar, even the feel. I wonder how common these are. Judging by the craftsmanship, I'd say it cost a small fortune.

I laugh, a man with a sword in one hand and a pistol in the other, a man of two eras. I wish I had a way to strap them securely to me, I can already feel my hands starting to cramp. "Wait..." I stare at my arms, holding them outstretched. "Where the yig are my tattoos?"

episode three

Like an idiot, I stand there in the middle of the dirt road, turning my forearms back and forth, as if my tattoos will suddenly reappear.

My head keeps shaking and my mouth keeps saying no, as my mind contemplates whether or not there's more than a foggy memory at play. Shooting a quick glance at the sky, I'm annoyed that there's nothing but wispy clouds, but I have no idea what I'm looking for.

Turning back to the road ahead, I notice some kind of scratches along the ground that lead to the wreckage. The jagged grooves aren't anything I recognize, nor is the spacing between them. It looks like something moved side to side as it advanced and then stopped ten feet before the levi.

I attempt to follow the grooves but quickly lose them, so I return to the wreckage and try again. I fail a second time. Crouching down, I run my fingers through the grooves, expecting them to tell me something, but there's nothing. Glancing about, I realize I've got no instinct or intuition giving me a hint. It's like I can't track anymore. Chewing on my lip, I stand. "What the yig can this body do?" I ask myself.

Snapping twigs draw my attention to three figures moving slowly in the underbrush on the north side. I shoot a quick glance to the south. It looks like I only have company on one front.

I try pulling the hammer back on the pistol, but it won't move. I turn it over, wondering where the bullets go. The only thing I see is a little switch, moving it back and forth doesn't open it up or anything. I could kick myself for not having checked it out properly as soon as I found it. The yigging thing could just be ornamental, put there to screw with the poor idiot who was ambushed and went for it.

With a steadying breath, I figure I might as well bluff. My new friends shouldn't be any the wiser, at least at first. Along with the short sword, I feel the odds are still in my favor.

I watch and wait as they slowly advance. It dawns on me that the three shambling, shadowy mounds in front of me are too close together, almost like they want me to step forward and focus on them. I quickly glance over my shoulder and see a much bigger one making its way towards me at a steady clip. Swiftly, I move south so that I can see them all at once. The big one immediately slows down.

Inexplicably, I start feeling pressure in my chest. I break into a sweat, my heart starts pounding. My breathing speeds up and I'm feeling jumpy. Is this excitement all it takes to make me fall apart? Nothing's happened yet! I've dealt with much worse than this, haven't I? I start yelling at them, more to distract myself from endless questions than anything else. "Come on, let's get going. I don't have all day."

They gradually get close enough for me to see that they're covered in ratty, brown blankets. Bits of worn boots or clothing peek out as they move. A smaller one trips on a hole in the road, and its covers fall off. Yig, it's a kid. Can't be more than ten, and probably hasn't ever seen a bath. What the yig is this, a family trying to rob me in slow motion?

Immediately, I point my pistol at the little guy and catch a glimpse of the medium-sized one flinching. "Hello mommy," I say with a sneer. They don't react. Something's wrong. The kid just puts his blanket back on, and they keep inching forward. I notice that there's a hole in the blanket near their faces, and its darkly stained below it.

As they close in, I hear them muttering to each other in a bizarre, guttural language of slurping and smacking sounds.

Suddenly, my chest feels like something is swelling in it. Yig, it's hard to breath. I flex my fingers, while trying not to lose my grip on the pistol. My head's bobbing with every sharp intake of breath. "Stop advancing or I'm going to start shooting."

"No," says the big one, with a voice so deep that he sounds like a mountain moving. He straightens up, his huge arms now visible. He is enormous and broad. Yig, he must have been nearly doubled over as he approached. In one hand is a well-worn hand-axe, looking like child's toy. The other hand is a huge clenched fist. In a slurred voice, and dragging out each word, he says, "Give... things."

I take a few steps back. "I'm keeping what I have, thanks. Now get out of here, before I start shooting." I'm gritting my teeth and blinking hard to ignore the pain. I feel like my chest just wants to burst open. Glaring at them as they stare back at me, each waiting for the other to make a move. As the pain sharpens, my head bobs for a second, and the big guy leaps at me.

The big guy's hand-axe swings unexpectedly close, as I barely manage to get my cold molasses of a body out of the way. I try to stab him with my short sword, but I nearly fall over instead. What the yig? I feel like I have no idea what I'm doing. The big guy takes advantage of the moment, and with a solid slap from his free hand, he sends my sword flying.

Suddenly my legs are pulled out from under me. The two smaller ones immediately climb on to my back. The pain inside me is making me dizzy. It's like my heart's being crushed and my pistol arm is on fire.

The medium one latches her fingernails into my pistol hand. I scream, but refuse to let it go. If I lose that, I've got nothing.

Glancing up, I catch the big guy winding up to bring his fists thundering down on my head. Blinking past the pain, I shrug the small ones off and roll towards the medium one just in the nick of time.

She and I roll and tussle. She keeps trying to bite my face, and I keep trying to put my pistol in her face to make her back off. Her eyes are wild and furious, I can't remember encountering people so raw and savage. I need a new strategy. She reaches for my eyes with those fingernails and I go with my gut instincts. I head-butt her, stunning her but in trying to scramble to my feet I fall back down onto all fours.

My head's spinning, my chest is screaming, and then a wave of nausea rides in on top of everything. I bite my lip hard to keep me focused on the present. As a second wave of nausea hits, I realize what's happening: magic's failing.

Glancing up, I see the big guy and the rest of his family stagger for a moment, thrown off by the lack of magic in the air. Their magical disguises melt away. Their skin creaks like old leather as it tightens, their eyes hollow, and one by one, they turn at look at me in a portrait of horror. The big guy roars, immediately followed by the others.

"I freaking hate ghouls." Taking a step backwards, I wobble, my arm jutting out to try and stabilize me. My vision starts to narrow and flashes of light start appearing. What the yig is going on? "No!" I yell at myself. "No freaking way I'm getting eaten. No way!"

As the big guy jumps at me, I point my pistol square at him and pointlessly pull the trigger. Suddenly all my pain and anxiety rushes from my core, through my arm, and out the pistol. In a fiery flash of blue, he drops. The kick-back is significant, but swiftly putting up my second hand to steady my aim, I drop the other ghouls without a second thought. Then, as suddenly as it came, the nausea passes and my heart is no longer trying to kick its way out of my chest. Magic is restored. Was all that connected? What the yig?

I run my hand through my hair, shaking my head in disbelief. "What just happened?" I stare at the pistol and then quickly scan about for any more of them.

Confident that I'm alone, I slowly approach the fallen ghouls. With my pistol pointed at their heads, I give them a nudge with my foot, and inspect the flaming wounds. It looks like they have been hit by flame strikes, as the wounds go clean through the body, are burn-sealed, and the edges have a small amount of blue flame.

Looking past them, I see two newly-splintered trees at the forest edge. "Freak me blue and call me a yigging idiot... How the yig did I do that?" That's when the lovely smell of the dead ghouls hits me, and I lose whatever it was I still had in my stomach after all this time.

After pulling myself back together, I find my short sword and take a last look at the bodies. The good news is that I've survived; the bad news is that I don't know if I can do it ever again.

episode five

Not having a better plan, I follow the winding road on and on, until my entire body is screaming for me to relent and at least sit and rest, if not sleep. Other than birds every now and then, I haven't seen any signs of life. I've also found nothing to eat, and my stomach's really not happy about it.

Coming over a small hill, I laugh with relief as the road mercifully offers up a large rock in a good spot. Climbing on top and satisfied that no one's going to get the jump on me, I sit. Immediately, I feel the full weight of my exhaustion and my body slumps. Putting the sword and pistol down right beside me has my hands celebrating. Rubbing them, I peer around, taking in my surroundings. Unfortunately, the road ahead looks exactly like the road I've taken, dirt hugged by desolate forest.

Staring at the road ahead, I say to myself, "Should I turn back? Maybe try to make it through the forest?" Scratching my beard, I peek up at the orangey-red sky. "Night's coming." Yig, I forgot about night. How dead do you have to be to forget about the night? I slap myself a few times to wake myself up. I don't like the prospect of finding ghouls, or worse, at night. Until I can figure out what's wrong with this body and why my head's not clearing up, I need to avoid trouble.

Sighing, I look at the flowers and plants near me. It's got to be summer. Closing my eyes, I try to figure out how far north I might be, and more importantly, how many hours of darkness I'm going to face and just how dark it's going to be, but... I've got nothing. Rubbing my forehead, I know I've got to press on. Every muscle and joint in my body protests as I pick up my sword and pistol and continue.

I keep my eyes peeled for any sign of a rabbit or a deer that I can turn into dinner. I figure sorting out how exactly I'd cook one will be a fun problem to have.

Several times I stop and prevent myself from looking back. Each time doubt creeps into my mind, I shrug it off, and keep putting one foot in front of the other. I remind myself that roads lead to places, they don't just happen. Therefore, stay with the road, and don't double back.

Two hours later, my feet are cursing my every step as I make my way up to the top of a large hill. I promise myself that I'll rest for a good long while. The sun's a thin red memory on the horizon, and the stars offer little other than a set of spectators for what's to come. Staring out at the darkened landscape, I notice something shining. Wait, there's several shiny things.

I crouch down quickly, not wanting to be seen. My mind goes through a few of the things it could be, from potential bandits to animals to water. My throat's parched and sore. I'd easily kill for some water.

A few minutes go by with no change, and an eerie silence. Wiping my forehead, I go back and forth between whether to risk going down there, or staying up here.

"Yig it. I'm too hungry to stay and too tired to care." I get up and carefully start down the hill.

A few yards into my descent, I realize there's no forest on this side of the hill, only stumps and a few withered trees here and there. I bend down to the dark grass. It feels strangely crunchy. "What the yig?"

With a firm tug, I pull some out of the ground and examine it up close. I glance up at the dark sky and then look about, but there's not enough light here to see this stuff properly. A chill runs down my spine when I rub it between my hands. It crumbles right away. It's got a filmy residue. Sniffing it, it smells like... dry. Weird. A snippet of a memory flashes by, something about a banquet hall and the smell of happiness wafting in.

There's definitely something mana related here, I

can feel it. I scratch my face again. What could have happened here to create such a wasteland? Whatever it was, it's probably long gone. At least, I hope so.

As I get closer, I see that the fleeting sunlight's been bouncing off levi-cars, lots of them, possibly hundreds. They're mostly in two rows, all pointing in the same direction — the direction I just came from. "Where were you going?" I wonder, and then I squint at them. "Maybe you were running from something."

Several of the levi-cars at the front are banged into each other. There are a dozen that went off the edge of the road and down into a ditch. I can't see any windshields and the two closest to me have puncture holes right through the roof.

Hesitating for a minute, I decide to run my hand along the roof of one of the levis. The paint feels old and mostly rough, with a few smooth parts. That was probably what I saw shining. "Maybe the roof holes happened after everyone was gone? How did you all just stop here, in the middle of nowhere?"

Squinting into a few of them, a chill runs down my spine. They're all still in gear, like the life was sucked out of them in an instant. "What the yig?" This is really starting to get under my skin.

Folding my arms, I lean against one of the levi-cars and stare up at the moon. It's so quiet, there are not even bugs calling out to each other. Gazing about,

I catch a glow in the distance and stand up straight, taking my pistol and sword off the roof. The fiery image goes out but the hair on the back of my neck goes up. Tilting my head and squinting hard, I wait for it. The glow reappears and seems to be wobbling and getting bigger. Yig.

Licking my lips, I look about in the falling darkness for somewhere to hide. Desperate, I climb quietly into one of the levis, cursing the door as it creaks.

My chest is getting that pressure again -- is that a good thing? I'm probably about to drop dead. Just what I need, dying in the middle of some freaky dead-zone because my head's all scrambled up. I tighten my grip on the pistol like it's my only hope of seeing the morning.

Now, I wait. I hate waiting.

episode six

I lay flat on my back on the floor of the levi-car. The seats are rotted and decayed into decrepit shadows of what was once luxury. I brace my feet against the side with my pistol clasped tightly in both hands.

The rushing sound of my own blood is driving me crazy. Each drop of sweat that falls onto the metallic floor nearly sends me into a panic. "Come on," I whisper to myself through clenched teeth.

As much as I'd like to imagine that it's nothing, or maybe someone walking around with an old-world torch, I know better. If I'm lucky, it's someone I can talk to, but more than likely, only one of us is going to be walking away from this.

I reaffirm my sweaty grip on the pistol for the millionth time, and shake my head, trying to stay focused and ready. My ears perk up as I pick up the sound of shuffling, back and forth. It sounds big judging by how long the shuffle seems to take. Then, there is the distinctive sound of claws scraping along the sides of a levi-car.

There's a screech that sounds like a thousand souls being ripped from their bodies. My blood goes ice cold. Even through my jumbled memories, I know a carn when I hear one. "No, no, no," I whisper to myself. "How the yig can I deal with a carn?" Shutting up and listening carefully, I hear it moving in very measured steps.

Think. Yig, it's mapping the area. They do that when they're alone and they're hunting for prey. At least that means it's alone. Not like I have a chance though, but I know I've got a minute to think.

I run a hand through my sweat-soaked hair. "Come on W—" My mind skids to a stop again. I almost felt like I had my name there. "Okay... What do I know? It's got skin that's yigging tough, a dead mage's skull to focus its mana, and..." There's some mess of thoughts about magical experiments but I can't make any sense out of it.

I suppress a laugh. "One huge, smart fire monster against my knife and pop-stick. No problem."

Carefully, I shift my body to give me a better look out the windshield. Pressure's building in my chest again, though thankfully there's no nausea, at least not yet. My hands are shaking like wind chimes in a tornado. This body's all wrong.

The darkness on the left side of my levi-car is

slowly pushed back as I catch a glimpse of the carn's fiery head. Orange and white flames surround its bleached skull. I watch as it lumbers into view, coming up to the levi-car in front of mine. With a mighty clawed hand, it caves in the roof. The metal frame whimpers as the carn rips it to pieces without a second though. A memory skids past me, something about being nearly burned alive by a carn. Was that me or a story I heard? Maybe something I saw, once? It doesn't matter, now I'm definitely not letting it get close to me.

Just then the carn's flames bloom outwards, arcing through the air and then coming together on that levi-car. I can see metal parts slowly surrender their form in the intense heat. The carn's not looking at it though, it's searching. It knows I'm here, and I think it wants me to watch the show. I hate freaking smart creatures.

I've held my breath so long I'm starting to see my own stars. The carn goes on to a levi further ahead, and I suck in as much air as I dare.

My stomach's turning into a raging knot of agony. I've got that watery feeling in my mouth. Yig, am I really going to puke now? What a way to die... Wait, that's not it. My eyes go wide as I realize what's about to happen. Yig it, I'm going for it.

Kicking open the levi-car door, I scramble out and skid to a stop, my pistol pointing straight at the carn's chest. It whips around and glares at me, the empty eye sockets of its mage-skull burning brightly with orange flame.

I swallow hard as I realize just how yigging huge these things are. It's over eight feet tall and muscular like a giant warrior with three-clawed hands. Its head sits on a strange looking black layer where a person's collarbone would be.

In the time it takes me to dash a few yards, the carn picks up a levi-car and throws it at me. I dive low to the ground and it sails over me. Rolling to my back, with both hands wrapped tightly around the pistol, I pull the trigger and... nothing happens.

"No!" I scream like a mother being ripped from her daughter. I keep pulling the trigger again and again. My stomach drops so hard and fast, I think I'm going to pass out. Just then, all that pressure in my chest races through my arm and out the pistol. Flaming blue balls shoot out the barrel and I'm thrown back. I catch a glimpse of the carn's flames dousing just before they hit. "Let's see how you do without any magical shielding, carny."

Scurrying back to my feet and snatching my pistol off the ground, I keep my eyes on the bent over carn. I take a second to shake out my fingers and wrist, which feel like I've stabbed a hundred needles in them.

The carn lurches to one side, then the other. It

drops to one knee, but clearly isn't dead. With a moan, it stands back up, a claw covering a burnt part of its chest. As its flames come back to full strength, it emits a sound that feels like a laugh. I don't need to think about my stomach to know that magic's back. "Yig me."

I point the pistol at it again. Without thinking or hesitation, I'm surprised to see another blue shot come out, knocking the carn on its heels. With a quick glance at the levi-car where I'd left my short sword, I decide I've got only one chance and bolt in the direction the levis had come from. I have no idea what I'm doing or where I'm going, except that I'm not going to get ripped apart and burned to death by the carn, not today.

episode seven

I fall down and lie there in the middle of the road. My feet refuse to take me any further, and I can't blame them. I reneged on our agreement, after all. I shield my eyes from the brutal early morning sun. "I should wake up any minute night, right? In a nice bed with breakfast sausage smells and everything, right?" I'm disappointed no one answers. There'd be some solace in knowing I'd gone crazy. At least I'd have company.

Sitting up, I glance over my shoulder at the dusty road. There's a mile of nothing. Still, I doubt I've killed it. There wasn't a single shot that had gone clean through it. Tough yig, that thing.

Grunting like a broken, old man, I start to stand up but then abandon the idea half-way. My arms perched on my knees, I squint up at the sky. I have a feeling like I'm looking for something, but I don't know what. I can't even remember who I wanted revenge on or why. Did I even know after I came back to life this time? Even my recent memories feel strangely fuzzy. Looking at my arms, I wonder why I so desperately want those tattoos to reappear. "Gah!" I scratch my head hard and then pick up a rock and throw it at the desolate wasteland. "Stupid yigging crap."

Smoothing down my beard, I find a few stowaway pebbles and twigs. I don't know why, but I start chuckling. It feels good to laugh. Rubbing my face with my rough and dusty hands, I decide it really is time to get up. Yig, I would kill for something to drink or eat. My throat feels like a carn is crushing it.

Peeking up at the blazing sun again, it dawns on me that I need to be smarter. There's no telling how long it's going to take me to find some civilization or water. Pulling off my shirt, I wrap the filthy thing around my head.

I imagine what I must look like: a wild eyed, shirtless bandit with a long-barreled pistol. The blood-stained brown pants and shoes a beggar might throw away really add that special something. I stare at the long road I've already covered and think back to the carn and my sword. I shouldn't have left that behind.

With an arched eyebrow, I stare at the eerie scenery: the weird, melted, brown grass, withered trees and dusty roads. There are some scorched outlines along the ground at the road-side, almost like reminders of buildings long gone. Licking my cracked lips, I shrug. I'm not up for investigating it. I've got one thing on my mind, the short sword.

Staring at the long road back, I get butterflies thinking about the carn. I was lucky to get away once, what are the chances I can do that twice? I'm certain that if I don't go back for the sword now, I'll have lost it forever. But the chances of finding food and water along the path back are zero. "GAH!" I scream at the top of my lungs. Instead of relief, I just get a scratched throat. I need to stop being an idiot.

Grudgingly, I start walking back to find my short sword. Every few steps I stop and rethink what I'm doing, and each time, I give myself a mental kick to keep going.

It's afternoon by the time the long line of abandoned and broken levi-cars come into view. I approach carefully, shaking my pistol arm every now and then, as if I had to stop it from nodding off. There's no sign of the carn. While I believe they're nocturnal, you never know when one's decided to pull an all-nighter. Like everyone, I've heard stories. Like everyone, I have no idea whether or not they're true.

The sight of the levi-cars is even more unnerving in daylight. What looked like fairly straight lines abandoned reasonably peacefully, is far from it. Most are smashed into each other, looking like they were trying to break the line and get around the person ahead of them. Some of the ones in the ditch look like they were desperate to go anywhere, fast. Something must have descended upon them quickly.

I notice a lot of strange black mounds near the cars, each one about the size of two handfuls of dirt. They start a few yards before the first one, and radiate around them no more than a dozen yards.

My curiosity gets the better of me, and I crouch down and examine one. It looks like fused darkly-colored glass beads, but it's got a strange odor. I stand back up and abandon the idea of finding a stick to poke it with or touching it. With my luck, there'd be a storybook demon inside. I find myself staring up at the sky again. Other than a few dense clouds in the distance, there's just blue, blue and more blue.

With a sigh, I start searching the first couple of levis, not sure which one I was in last night. I thought it'd be easy, but memory is a weird thing. After searching my fifth one, I start to feel anxious. "Did that yig take off with my sword? What the yig would a carn want it for, a trophy?"

I give myself a slap. "Stop being an idiot. Just keep looking," I tell myself. Hopefully, this time I'll listen.

The sixth levi-car comes with an unexpected surprise. Strapped to the back of it is a damaged, but still sealed, woven traveler's picnic trunk. It's a big, brown rectangle of beaten-up beauty.

I cry with laughter as I confirm that the magical

seal is still intact. Of course, I can't open it, but fingers crossed, I can get it open the next time magic fails. Seconds have never felt like days so badly in all my life. I keep switching from fantasizing about what's inside, to trying to brace myself for the massive disappointment I'm sure is lurking inside.

I try to search around some more for my sword, but like a moth to a flame, I can't leave the picnic trunk. If I'm more than three steps away, I get panicky that I'll miss my chance at opening it. The only thing to do is wait. I really hate waiting.

After what feels like two hours, I start to worry about what'll happen if the sun goes down, the carn comes back, and magic's still humming along. I can't fathom abandoning the trunk. Staring at the blood stains left behind by the carn, I remember they have great memories and will hunt down those that have wronged them. I'm sure I'm high up on that carn's list of people to revisit soon.

I pace back and forth in front of the trunk when it finally dawns on me, I'm an idiot. I can cut the straps and drag that beauty around with me. Provided I find my sword, I should be able to open it when the time comes.

Glancing up at the sun, I figure I have more than enough time to get safely away. And if magic drops while I'm getting myself organized, I should be okay.

With a renewed sense of purpose, I scramble about until I finally find my short sword. I find its tip poking out from under a levi-car, just enough to catch my eye. It makes short work of the straps and I start dragging it off. I keep telling myself its full of treasure, but at the back of my mind, I'm afraid it'll have a body, or worse, be empty.

I stop myself from biting at the woven trunk a third time. My lip is still bleeding from the last stupid attempt. Frustrated and unable to help myself, I scream and punch it. I'm lucky I don't cut my knuckles. I really need to stop being an idiot.

It's been a few hours, and I'm tired and starved. Rubbing my dirty face, I walk around the trunk. I keep telling myself it's just sitting there in the middle of the dusty road, that it's not actually mocking me, but part of me doesn't agree. "Come on!" I yell it and then the sky. Finally, I throw my hands up and slump down beside the trunk. Leaning against it, I stare out at the bleak surroundings.

It doesn't take long for the landscape to start making me angry, with its deceptive hills offering hope and promise on the other side, only have more scorched earth instead. My leg's bouncing with impatience. I stop short of telling it to stop, realizing every time I talk to myself I'm probably taking another step closer to the cliffs of insanity. To distract myself, I yell at the few clouds that float by. They ignore my taunts… cowards.

Finally, I feel it happening, that nausea in the pit of my stomach. With tears of joy, I spring to my feet and snatch my short sword out of the ground, tossing my pistol aside. I check twice to see that the seal still has its magical shimmer, not wanting to accidentally have my blade bounce off again and stab me in the face or something. Dying by my own hand in the middle of nowhere is not on my list of things to do.

Staring at the seal, I wait, my leg bouncing maniacally. My fingers twitch as fantasies about what's in the trunk keep going through my head: maybe it's got a feast or maybe a flying machine.

My nausea hits its peak, but the seal doesn't look any different. "Ah…" I glance around, not sure what I'm looking for. "Screw it! I'm going for it!" I yell, tears rolling down my face. Licking my lips, I carefully slice my sword right through the seal. I stab my blade into the road and thrust my arms up in victory. "YES!"

Clapping my hands together, and with a huge grin on my face, I take hold of the lid and pull, the whole trunk moves as one piece. "What the?" I put it down and stare at the seal. It's untouched. "It's *got* to have a crystal battery, but where?" I turn it over, finding nothing. "There's no telling how much mana it has left. YIG!"

With a mighty, two-handed heave, I pull my short sword out of the ground, cursing myself, and cut the seal again. Right before my eyes, I watch it re-seal. "What kind of yigging idiot made this yigging thing? GAH!!" I drop my sword and run my hands through my hair as I pace about. As the sensation in my stomach starts to ease, my anxiety just goes up and up.

I kick the trunk, screaming. It rolls with complete disregard. "GAH!!" I pull at my hair and beard, feeling myself teetering on the edge of madness.

"Something, there's got to be. Yes!" I pick up my sword and jam it into the seal, and then I kick the hilt for everything I'm worth. The trunk goes end-over-end, and my sword flies off.

I hop around screaming, clutching my bleeding foot. After finding my sword and stroking the etchings at the base of the blade, I sigh in relief as the wounds heal. Cursing myself, I have to use both hands to pull my blade out of the ground. Turning back to the trunk, it's unharmed and worse, unopened.

"I can't take this." I crumple to the ground and cry, my head in my hands. My nose oozes and my mouth is gummy and pasty. I'm gazing at the vicious trunk when I notice some engraved symbols shining on the seal in the sunlight. Taking hold of the seal, I rotate it until it's lines look like clouds. "Why not?" I try opening it. The lid moves a little, but enough that the seal isn't a concern anymore.

Laying down, I get my fingers and feet under the lid and put my back into it. The trunk rips open, the lid coming clean off and the few contents fly out. I dive for a fist-sized red bobble.

Laughing and crying, I whisper to it, "Hello apple." I turn it around delicately on my grimy fingertips. It's lumpy with green and yellow patches in places, but perfect. I sniff it. A smile cracks across by my face as I relish how it even smells like food.

I sit there in the middle of the road, not sure what to do, coveting my prize. A sadness falls over me as I realize that if I eat the apple, then I'll be alone again; my hunger and the apple will be gone. "That's messed up," I say, giving myself a slap. "Come on, shake off that stupid thinking."

Out of the corner of my eye, I spot something small moving. Tossing the apple, I dive for my pistol and point it at the tiny brown thing, my heart beating a mile a minute. "It's just a freaking mouse..." Summoning the remnants of my once powerful self, I snatch the little mouse up by its tail and stare at it. "Not so terrifying now, are you?" Shaking my head, I drop my pistol and lay the mouse on my hand. "How did you survive in that trunk?" Glancing about, I laugh. "Maybe you've just been living out here, but if you have, then you're probably going to try and kill me like everything else I've run into." I squint intently at the mouse. "Are you a him or her? Let's go with him."

He wiggles his nose in the air, and then turns his head away from me.

Frowning, I put him on the ground in front of me. I lay myself on the ground, prone, and stare at him.

The mouse stares back, and offers a delicate squeak.

I look at the apple and nod, not sure if I'm imagining things or if I somehow understood something. Without hesitation, I bite off a small piece and gently put it beside the mouse.

"Here you go. Oh, you're welcome, Randmon," I say with a smile. I rub my head wondering where the name came from, and why I'm talking to a mouse.

Watching the mouse inspect the chunk of apple engrosses me. After sniffing and moving around it, then sniffing it some more, he decides to give it a nibble. Satisfied, he gobbles it up.

A sense of freedom washes over me, and I bite into the apple with a ridiculous amount of force, nearly slicing my tongue in the process. Closing my eyes, I let the rich sweetness and bitterness play on my tongue, and revel in the joy of having something to crunch and swallow. Before I know it, I've eaten it, core and all.

The mouse looks up at me, and I feel guilty. "I'm sorry, Randmon. That's all I've got." Why am I talking to the mouse? Hey, I forgot about the other stuff!" Rubbing my hands together, I get up to check out the other treasures that had spilled out of the trunk. There's a folded wad of thick paper that looks like a map, an empty coin purse, and an odd steel canister.

I stash the map, ignore the purse and shake the canister next to my ear. It makes an encouraging whooshing sound. Glancing back at the trunk and then at Randmon, I figure that the enchantment on the trunk must have kept everything suspended, similar to how my sword works for preserving me.

Feeling both ends, I finally find a part that turns. I scream as water starts to spill out. Flipping it over, I splash some into my mouth. Sealing it back up, I dance about like a triumphant idiot until I lock eyes with the mouse. "I didn't know! Have you seen one of these before? Anyway, there's still some in there. Don't worry."

Afraid I'll spill it all, I carefully turn the lid. I pour some into my hand and let Randmon get his fill. The rest quickly disappears into me.

I lay back, still in the middle of the road, and gaze up at the late afternoon sky. Putting Randmon on my chest, I chuckle as he snuggles in. "Life's not so bad." I yawn, feeling the full weight of my exhaustion. Glancing to each side, I figure I'll just catch a quick nap; it's not like there's anyone around.

episode nine

There's nothing like being wrenched from sublime slumber and thrust into the land of the awake by a boot to the face.

As I roll over on the road, I feel hands trying to yank my shirt off my head. Getting to all fours, I glance up. There are three blurry forms moving about, at least one of them is laughing at me.

I wipe my bloody face. My nose is just short of broken, but that won't stop me from breaking each of theirs or worse.

As I get up, they spread out. One of them has her hands down and free, another's got a knife, and third's got their hands behind their back. They're dressed in dark dusky pants, and matching hooded shirts that tied in the front. They've probably been working together for a bit, learned some lessons the hard way.

One of them winds up for another kick. I start backing up, playing it as if I'm wobbly. I dart sideways and catch the leg, and though I want to twist and break it, my body has no idea what to do. Under the hood I see a blond haired woman with a scarred face. As I stand there like an idiot, she lands a punch to my jaw and I drop to my knees.

She laughs and says something I don't understand, then backs up.

Looking up at her, I rub my jaw. A nibble of fruit and a slurp of water, and I let myself come undone. I see the trunk behind them. Glancing down, I confirm that my sword and pistol are missing. I'm furious with myself. "Nice job, idiot," I mutter under my breath.

Studying them for a second, I realize they could have killed me in my sleep, but didn't. Maybe they wanted to have some fun, maybe they're looking for a new member of their crew.

Not having a better plan, I figure I might as well let them think that I'm done, and track them later. I drop to the ground and pretend I've passed out.

Through the thinnest of eye slits, I watch as they debate and then pick up my trunk and start walking off. Just as they start to pass out of sight, I panic. "Oh freaking Mother of Mercy, I don't know how to track anymore!" Scrambling to my feet, I glance about for Randmon, whispering to him. He's not here. Maybe he caught a ride on the trunk. For a second, I wonder if I just imagined him and then shake off the thought.

I've got to get moving. It doesn't take long for them to notice me.

The tallest one of them immediately turns, their hands disappearing behind their back again. Frowning, I remember I didn't get a peek at what that one's hiding. It could be some real trouble. "Hey!" I yell at them, waving. Yeah, the crazy man wants more. No way I'm letting you guys leave me with absolutely nothing in the middle of this place.

They start talking to each other as I slowly approach. I must look like a real prize: bloody shirt around my head, tanned skin, ratty beard, a mop of shoulder length hair, and wild, driven eyes. I wasn't a threat when they ambushed me, and I'm sure they're trying to figure out if I'm one now. Maybe they're debating if I could be of some value. Just let me get a little closer, I'll show you some value.

As I walk towards them, the shortest one approaches. It's not the leader, judging by the body language of the other two. I keep my hands palm up until I'm close enough to recognize it's the blond. Like a kid bolting with a stolen prize, I knock her flat with my shoulder and dash past. I catch a glimpse of her head whipping around, a look of frustrated surprise on her face.

As the tall one pulls a small crossbow out, his hood slips back. The guy's a real piece of work, broken nose and brown hair that looks like it was cut by a blind man with the shakes. I'm able to close the gap before he's got the bolt loaded, and I plow into him, sending him crashing to the ground and the crossbow skidding along the ground. With both fists, I hammer down on his chest, leaving him winded.

The leader's one step ahead of me, and has my pistol pointing straight at my head. Her hood's sitting back enough that I can see the woman clearly, and there's something about her eyes that tell me she knows what she's holding. *Can she use it* is a question I'm not eager to answer.

Screw it, I decide to go for broke and charge her.

She's about to shoot when she lowers the pistol and stares at me in disbelief. "Weslek?"

I skid to a stop and stare at her, panting. Weslek? What's... wait, that means something. Maybe it's my name?

"Weslek?" she asks insistently, her hand outstretched and hovering inches from my chest.

The other two are up and itching to take me down. Licking my lips, I smile and nod at the leader.

She gives me a friendly slap on the arm, the others relax.

I have no idea who this woman is.

As we start walking down into the valley, the leader points to a levi-car left by a tree and says something. We all start heading toward it. The closer we get, the more I keep asking myself why they left it there, it looks like it's levitating just fine. Ah, I see why. The scratch marks on the front and the dent.

Standing back as they strap the trunk on the back and chat, I glance around. There's no danger around, so I'm willing to bet that when magic stopped, they lost control and hit the tree.

Thinking of magic, I look up at the greying sky. Something about it and the diffused rays of the sun remind me of something... a floating city. I've seen one, in a sky like this. Seen the magic driven machines, keeping it aloft. I wonder what happened to it, the first time magic failed? No magic, no connecting to the mana of the world, and no natural conversion from life force to mana and back.

"Weslek!" yells the guy, wrenching my attention to the present. He motions for me to get in the levi-car's backseat with him. I get in.

It's a bit cramped and less comfortable than I expect, but the idea of not beating my feet into a thin paste is more than welcome.

The leader starts the levi up. It shakes and rises like a drunk standing up. The engine sounds worse for wear, under the out of sync warbling noises there's a deep hum. Once we start moving, I don't care.

Before I know it, I drift off. It feels like I've only been asleep for a few minutes when my head roughly smacks against the side of the levi. I barely have time to duck my head and cover it with my arms before the car flips over and slides. Smashed glass flies around all of us.

Something tells me it's not magic failing this time.

episode eleven

My head's spinning. Squinting at the sky, I see that it's dusk. One of the women is moaning in the front seat. I can't turn my head to see the guy, but he's not making any noise. That's not good.

A quick check tells me nothing's broken, but everything hurts. There's some blood from somewhere, but I'm not overly concerned. Still, I'd like to get my hands on my short sword and make sure. Unable to see it, I decide to crawl out on my hands and knees; shards of glass bite me for the privilege, drawing some crimson tax as I pass over them.

I can hear something large approaching, so I stay low and scan the surroundings. We're on yet another dirt road with a dense forest on one side and green fields on the other. There are no weapons lying nearby the crashed levi-car, and judging by the scratch-thump sound of whatever's heading our way, I'm going to need some help. My hands are already slick with sweat.

I poke my head back in and see the leader stirring. Picking through the tossed debris, I still don't find my pistol or sword. There's a distinctive screech from behind me and my blood runs. "carn?" Then comes a second one, its pitch just different enough to make my heart skip a beat. Wiping my face, I stare at the ground. "What did I do to deserve *two*?"

A few seconds later, they lumber into view. Their orange and white flames are burning brightly, and their mage-skulls seem to be almost sliding back and forth on their black necks. One of them notices me and its skull's eyes light up. It's got a burnt, black scorch mark on its chest.

A fatalistic laugh escapes me and I hang my head. "I guess I'm at the top of your revenge list. Nice to know it's personal," I say, shaking my head. I grab the leader and shake her vigorously until she smacks my hands away. A glint of a small knife in the backseat. Thank you, carn, for the extra light.

Heaving the unconscious guy aside, I reach over and grab the knife. In a blink, I'm outside, cutting the straps off the trunk, thankfully to have the levi between me and the two carnu.

Tossing aside some of their things, I grab my pistol and short sword. Randmon's in there too, nibbling something. He stops and looks up at me.

"Okay, come on," I say, picking him up and

putting him on my shoulder. Crouching down and leaning against the levi-car, I try to come up with a plan that doesn't involve running as fast as I can and simply hoping that the scarred carn kills them first, instead of chasing after me. "I know it'll come after me, and that's why it's a bad plan," I tell Randmon.

Sometimes that little guy gets on my nerves, the little know-it-all. Stroking the middle of my forehead with my pistol, I realize I've got nothing else, other than a slightly less stupid plan. If the others don't get up soon, we're all going to burn. "Okay, what do you think? Go for it? Just whose side are you on?" Randmon jumps down.

Poking my head into the back of the levi-car, I tell them, "Get up. I'm going to distract them. You've got one shot to get out."

I close my eyes and try to connect with that pressure in my chest, but it's not there; not even a hint of pain. I chew on my lip wondering if maybe I'm just getting more used to it. It hurt like a yigging donkey kick in the chest at first, then it was just pressure. Maybe it's there. No time like the present to find out.

With a nod to Randmon, I bolt for the forest, yelling to get the carnu's attention. I don't have to look to know that they're staring at me, wondering what I'm doing. I run a dozen yards into the trees before sliding to the ground and peeking back at what's happening.

The new carn is heading for me, glancing about to see if it's a trap. But then the scarred one grabs it by the shoulder and growls and clicks at it. They've got a language... a freaking language. I bang my head against the dirt... freaking smart walking nightmares. My gut tells me the carnu are going to make sure the others are dead before hunting me down. They don't want to get outflanked.

Kneeling, I see that I've unconsciously used the short sword to heal my wounds. I better be careful with that; I don't remember how to recharge the yigging thing.

I plant the sword in the dirt and take the pistol in both hands. With one eye closed, I try to focus my aim but it feels like my hands are just having fun mocking me. I watch the pistol tracking all over the place. Taking a steadying breath, I pull the trigger. Nothing happens. Mother of Mercy, can't something go my way? There's nothing going on inside me. How does this stupid thing work?

The scarred carn growls and they take up positions around the levi. Hoping I've given the others enough time, I pick up my sword and turn to the toppled levi-car. The leader's standing on top of it, her hood pulled back. She's got a bloody nose, a bleeding cheek, and fiery red eyes. With well-practiced calm, she's gesturing delicately and precisely in the air, mouthing words. An image of standing in a stone hall with dozens like her doing the same thing flashes in my mind. Who is she?

I hurry to her side, coming up from behind so as to avoid the carn taking a swipe at me. Climbing up, I point my pistol at the scarred carn. It's flame flares for a second. "I love you too, sunshine," I say with a grim smile.

There's something at the back of my mind, a voice and words. I give the woman a glance, and it's like I'm hearing her mutterings but it's in the voice of a demonic child. I almost slip off as I recoil, something in my deep memory making me momentarily afraid.

A red haze appears, surrounding the levi-car. I stare in surprise at the woman. Her eyes are glowing, and I swear I can feel the rush of mana flowing from the air, through her and then doing her bidding. I'm certain she's been part of a Wizard's inner circle. The heart shaped face, the sharp features, it's not from any realm or domain I can recall but her skill and confidence speaks volumes.

I turn my attention back to the carnu who have their clawed hands outstretched, testing the edge of the barrier. They're spreading out, talking to each other.

"Do you have a plan?" I ask her.

"Not really. You?"

I stare at her, stunned. "You can understand me?"

"How the yig can you understand me?" I repeat. It doesn't make any sense, why is she doing this now? Wait... I glance at the protective shield she's got up and the amount of concentration on her face, maybe she's not responsible for understanding me now. Why's this happening now? I run my hand through my sweaty hair and then shake my head. Who the yig cares, there's carnu.

Glancing back into the levi-car, I see the blond woman's stirring. I offer her a hand and help her climb out. I notice three scars on her face that are very distinctive. They remind me of ones that some types of severe criminals get, but I don't remember anything else.

"Can you wield magic like her?" I ask, pointing at her friend. I'm pretty sure I know the answer.

She stares at me confused. "Pan ji?"

"Wait. Can you understand me?"

She squints and rolls a hand at me. Maybe that means so-so.

I point at the other passenger. "What about the guy?"

Her face goes tight and steely. "Not making go."

Twisting my head to the side, I swear I understood some of that. "He's not going to make it? Is that what you meant?"

She nods.

"Great, we had too many anyway. No point in winning the easy way," I mutter. I catch a glimpse of Randmon on my shoulder, his little mouse face has a peculiar look that gets my attention. "Are you doing this language stuff?" He stares at me like an idiot. Right, a mouse is a mouse is a mouse. I turn back to the blonde as she fishes about in the levi, likely for some weapons. "Hey! What's her name?" I glance over at the acolyte, and she's dropping beads of sweat the size of marbles. We don't have a lot of time.

"Ania." She taps on her chest, "Dila."

"You're Dila, she's Ania, got it. I'm..." Yig, my brain just skids to a stop again, "I'm going to come up with a plan." I rub my forehead trying to think of what our options are. "Oh yig, no..." That freaking nausea's starting again. "Dila, magic's going to fail again."

"What?" she asks, preparing a crossbow.

I wave at the sky. "Magic, all magic, it's going to stop working in a minute," I say, trying to fend off outright panic.

Dila stares at me like I just said something crazy, because in her reality, I did. Who the yig can feel magic coming and going, it must sound like I can feel clouds moving in a foreign country. I bet they didn't know why their levi-car crashed into the tree.

Ania groans in pain, her footing slipping on the top of the levi for a second. The two carnu are pushing on her protective shield from opposite sides. Freaking smart fire-heads.

Concern flashes on Dila's face, "She no do—"

"Not doing well? Yeah, I can tell." With stupidly hopeful eyes, I look at Dila and ask, "Can you help her?"

She looks at our protector and shakes her head, "No." She puts the crossbow down, likely waiting for the shield to drop. I shake my head, realizing that if it were me, I would have shot and probably killed one of us by accident. They've clearly worked together before.

Dila pulls open her shirt, showing an under-layer of leather armor festooned with throwing knives. She's also got them along discreet slots on her thighs and upper arms. Yig, I had no idea.

Looking down at my pistol, I laugh. If Dila thinks that a crossbow and knives are going to have a chance against the carnu, she's way out of her league. So that leaves me with two options: try to take down the carnu, or try to get out of here faster than them. Given how Ania's at least an acolyte, that makes the second option almost as bad as the first.

Ania's groans of pain are becoming growls. It's only a matter of time before she's outright screaming and then she'll drop. The nausea in my stomach is building, but I've got no feeling of pressure to feed the pistol.

I find myself staring at the one tree that's inside the shield for some reason. Glancing about, I note how it's more of a strange oval now. As Ania screams, I watch as the tree withers right before my eyes. Startled, I step back and bang into Dila. "Transforming life force into mana... Did she just do that?" I grab Dila by the shoulders and point at Ania. "Did she just kill that tree?"

"Eat for mana," replies Dila.

Right, some people *can* do that. Wizards, acolytes and... gah, I had it. Huh. Staring at the withered tree, I think of the landscape. It looks really similar. Blue veins start to pop out on Ania's red face.

I close my eyes and concentrate on my heart and core. Come on, where's that raging beast that ran out my arm and pistol when I needed it? My eyes dart about desperately, I'm like a burning man looking for a barrel of water. I don't have much time until Ania goes down.

A whiff of an idea hits me, and my body reacts before I know what's going on. I watch myself drop my pistol and short sword, and shove Dila aside. As I haul the unconscious guy half out of the levi-car, she starts getting back up, fury in her eyes. I rip his shirt and put a hand square on his bare chest, while my other hand grabs my pistol. She's starting to scream at me.

Ania notices what I'm doing but can't react without dropping the protective shield. Dila's reaching for a knife on her thigh, screaming at me. Closing my eyes, I feel my nausea peak and... and then something else.

"AHH!!!!" I scream as the wounded man's essence burns up into my arm and then into my chest. It's like inhaling a hurricane, it's beyond agony. My jaw's clenched so tightly I expect my teeth to shatter any minute. Memories start hitting me so hard I'm on the verge of passing out. I have no idea if they're mine or his. Wrapping my arms around myself, tremors start, giving way to full convulsions. The one thought screaming through my head, over the deafening sound of the inner hurricane, is to hang on. Was that what the Old Man used to say?

Dila's face is red with rage. Her knife narrowly misses me as I flail about. She dives for my short sword, yelling "FARKES WESLEK!" In a single heartbeat, she rolls up to me and is poised to drive the sword through my throat. In a flash, she drops to the ground, a huge hole through her middle, my pistol streaming blue smoke. The convulsions are done.

Ania screams, her eyes wild with fury. The shield vanishes and she turns, glaring at me, both hands outstretched. Nothing happens. "Sorry lady, magic's not here right now. You've got to have your own mana, and you're all out."

I point my pistol at the scarred carn, shifting my gaze back and forth between them and Ania. The scarred carn says something to the other, motioning at the dead blond. To my surprise, they start backing up and then take off. Whatever the reason, I'm sure I haven't seen the last of them.

I'm feeling woozy, like a leaky bucket. Maybe I can't keep that much mana... or maybe... I don't know... doesn't really matter right now. If I'm not careful, I'm sure Ania's going to take the opportunity to leave a flaming blue hole right through me. Trying to stand, I stumble, grabbing the side of the levi-car, but keeping my pistol arm up and pointed at Ania the whole time. She's pacing about trying to assess the situation, her eyes going back and forth between me and her dead friends and the carnu retreating into the distance.

Looking back at the guy I drained, I lose it, throwing up. He's ghastly thin, with empty black eye sockets, and dark, matte skin that looks like burnt paper. His facial expression is something that will haunt me for days, if not weeks, I'm sure.

"Hey," I say to Ania as she sits down on the road, shaking her head. She doesn't look furious anymore, but there's no sign of sorrow or loss either. Maybe they hadn't worked together that long, or maybe they weren't friends. "I didn't mean to kill her. She came at me, and I didn't have a choice. The shield was going down in a minute, and... I didn't even know I could do that."

Licking my lips, I wait. The hurricane in my chest was halved by the shot and has been dropping, but I'm sure I've still got enough left in the tank for a good shot or two, perhaps more.

She gives me a blank look and shrugs, tapping her ear.

Furrowing my brow, I lower my pistol, doing a quick scan in case the carnu had doubled-back through the forest. All is quiet. I take a deep breath.

"Weslek..." I say, trying to make sense of the word. It feels like I've almost got it.

"Jargee Ma-na, weslek?" asks Ania, standing up and coming over. Her hands are palm up. I reaffirm my grip on the pistol as she approaches. The glint of the sun off my short sword tells me it's not far away.

She points at my free arm and motions like she wants to touch it. I do a gut check. As far as I know, magic's not working, but as far as I know, she could burn me alive with a touch. I can't feel Randmon on my shoulders, so I decide to roll the dice and see what happens. I give her a nod.

Immediately, she slaps her hands on my arm, her

eyes narrow. A memory snaps into place, and I shove her backwards. I point my pistol at her head. "Jargee Ma-na... yeah, I still have mana. That's Banarese. Yig, you were going to try and leech that right out of me? Your dying friend surrendered it to me, no way I'm giving you anything. What type of acolyte are you, anyway?"

Raising her hands slowly, a guilty smile crosses her face. "I had to try. I'd never attempted it before," she says, her accent noticeable this time. "So, what now?"

I stare at the ground and take a deep breath. A sense of relaxed calm is setting in. "I need to get to Banareal," I tell her, giving her a sideways look. I'm not sure what the place is, but it popped into my head when she touched me, along with the translation. I figure it's as good of a place as any.

"The floating city? Interesting. Why would you go there?"

Frowning, I ask, "Hey, how come you can understand me now, but not earlier? Is it Randmon? Where *is* that mouse?"

"Is that him?" she asks pointing behind me.

I spin around searching for that yigging mouse, and then I feel it. My back erupts in pain as flames shoot all around me. I'd missed the cue, magic's back and I turned my back like an idiot.

Landing on all fours, hanging on to consciousness by my fingernails, I scramble over for my short sword. After swiping the etched markings, I spin around ready with my pistol. She's levitating with a green sphere around her. She waves, and with a boom and rush of wind, she blurs away.

I eye the forest and the road in front and behind me. Tapping my short sword against my head, I notice it's glowing blue and I feel empty inside. Huh, I wonder if it healed me and took my mana to recharge itself.

I walk over to Dila's corpse and crouch down. She looks almost normal, except for the huge, burned hole right through her. I glance over at Mister Withered, unable to look at him for more than a second. There's something disturbingly familiar about the withered one, like I've seen hundreds before.

Staring at Dila, another translation wiggles loose from my memory. "Farkes weslek, eh?" I say, with a biting smile. "Well, if I hadn't been a *traitorous mana battery*, then I wouldn't know what you'd said, and we'd *all* be dead." I check her things, but everything's melted. Even the rings on her fingers are ruined.

I stare off in the direction I think Ania went. "You'll be back some day, won't you? How many of us are there out here? How many wesleks are you going to run into?" I can't figure out why she wanted me to come along. Maybe she was planning on leeching from me? Can she actually do that? I remember her touching my forehead and raise my rough hands to feel it, wondering if there's a marking or something.

I remember something... with the Old Man... I look at the ground, squinting. There was a Wizard and he touched me, draining me. But I recall the pain and agony, and then that moment... that moment where I pulled his energy into me. I look down the road where I last saw Ania. "Did you know I killed him? That I'm a wizard killer?"

episode fourteen

With a guttural yell, I heave the crashed levi-car over. It lands with a crunch, and sits there on the ground, a tired, beaten up lump of metal. I rummage through it, retrieving my map and taking a strap I can use as a belt. It'll keep my short sword at my side instead of in my hand. Funny how little things can feel like a luxury in the right moment.

I hear a squeak and turn to Randmon, who's on my shoulder. "Good to know you're okay." Seeing him, I feel a bit guilty for having lost track of him in all the action. Part of me wonders if he was on my shoulder all along. I give him a little rub on his furry brown back. He's smiling, I know it.

Hanging my head, I mutter, "I must be going crazy." I give Randmon a sideways glance, chuckle and add, "Yeah. At least the weather there is good."

I scout the area quickly for the carnu, then circle back to the levi. Chewing on my lip, I recall a bit of how it works. I hunt around for the engine panel, finding it on the back. It takes me some time to figure how to get the scratched up, protective cover off. Putting it down carefully, I sit and stare at the marvel behind it. There are three blackened discs, lined-up beside each other. The sapphire tubing around it has cracked, and the cloth webbing that connects everything is scorched brown in places. "It must have sparked and burned when we crashed." I run my finger along the mana-residue-covered webbing. "Probably already had some cracked tubes from the previous crash into the tree." Rubbing my forehead, I attempt to pull something helpful from the molasses of my mind. I almost have something and then it's like it disappears, as if magically pushed away.

Glancing up at the sun, I know that I've already pushed my luck with how much daylight remains. I lay the map out on the ground and lean over it. The notation's not familiar, and the landmarks drive me crazy. Twice I climb a tree, trying to get a better sense of where I am. According to the map I should have passed through a small town, but maybe I was asleep in the levi when we went through it? The best I'm able to do is get a rough idea of where I might be, and maybe which direction I should go. Folding up the map, I tuck it into the back of my pants, then make sure I've got my pistol and sword.

I look back at Dila and the guy I drained, immediately curing any sense of being hungry. I feel like I owe them some kind of apology. It's one thing if you mean to double cross people, and another if things just crash and burn. "For what it's worth, I didn't think it was going to work out this way. May you be well on your journey." Staring at the ground, I think about what happened for a moment, and then my hands do a wave that seems to come naturally but I don't recognize. Just who am I?

Taking a few steps, a worry hits me. Ania could show up with some friends and cause me real trouble. Maybe I should hide the bodies? No, I don't have time. Plus, there's the levi and it's not going to be easy to hide. Best to just get moving, and fast. I'll deal with Ania if and when she shows up. For all I know, it could be years before I see her again. Hopefully, I'm just one more person on her hate-list. But the carn, that's different. That's two encounters with the scarred one, and as the saying goes: there's never a second without a third.

Looking up at the dark sky, I decide it's best to try and sleep in the forest, hidden as best as I can be. I find an old oak tree whose roots create an alcove below it. Breaking the trunk into three pieces, I use them to shield me from obvious view. Given the distance from the road and the foliage around, hopefully I won't wake up to another kick in the head, or worse. With a reluctant sigh, I try to relax with my body as contorted as it is, and fall asleep.

The wet chill of morning comes too quickly.

Rubbing my face and scratching my beard, I finally come out of my hole and stand. My joints and muscles ache, but I'm alive. "Time to get moving."

By the time I come to a wooden sign post, the sun's drooping lazily in the sky. Like a kid seeing dad return from months at sea, I run to the sign. I don't care that the words are too faded to read, it's got an arrow. I pull out my map and confirm it's the right direction. "Maybe we've got some luck after all, Randmon." I check my shoulder, he's gone. Probably crawling around on me somewhere. He's a weird little guy.

Coming over a hill, I smile as I see rectangles of color and recently sowed fields. "Now we're getting somewhere." A barn comes into view and I yell and punch the air in triumph. But as I get closer, I realize its back side is burnt, and it's empty. A farm house comes up next, but that looks like a giant smashed it with a tree, if giants existed.

Sighing, I keep going. After a sparse forest, I come upon grassy fields to the south of the road and bare field to the north, with some crops growing in the distance. To my surprise, there's a person moving. He's wearing a large brimmed hat and clearly working.

"Hey!" I yell, waving a hand. Instead of waving back, he looks up and stares at me. I'm too far away to see clearly, but a chill runs through me. I glance around, catching sight of a few others standing in the field, all of them looking at me. I tighten my grip on my pistol and start moving again.

Given that they haven't run at me already, I'm fairly certain they're not ghouls. Mind you, there are more than a hundred other, worse things they could be. Part of me just wants to turn around and leave, but stubbornly I keep going. Maybe they're just normal people working. What type of an idiot would run screaming from normal people and into the flaming arms of carnu? Maybe they even know the way to Banareal. They've got to have heard of it.

Throwing a glance every now and then to the sides, I count twenty or so people working, all of them showing the same reaction. Maybe no one's just walked up to this place in a long time.

I come up to several buildings clustered together, eerily empty of people. "Welcome to the center of town," I mutter to myself, shaking my head. Standing there, I slowly notice that there are indeed people around, it's just they are standing so still, and in tight clusters, all of them dressed so plainly, that they blend right in to the faded gray wood of the buildings. There's probably a dozen... no, more.

Sweat's rolling down the middle of my back and making my pistol hand slick. I wipe my hand on my filthy, sweaty shirt, roll my shoulders, and crack my neck.

They're all just staring at me. No one's whispering or pointing, they're all just standing there, staring. It worries me that I've got no pressure or pain inside. Forcing a swallow, I keep my head down and walk.

One of the buildings I pass is boarded up, another looks like a general store of some kind but I can see its shelves are empty. What type of place is this?

Spotting what looks like a tavern, I head on over. If I'm going to have to fight my way out of this, I might as well get a drink and give them some restricted quarters. For some reason, I look down at my forearms hoping to see my tattoos have returned, but they haven't. I still don't know why I'm doing that, or why their return would help me. The Old Man would just tell me to rely on myself, not superstitious symbols or magical protection enchantments. For a moment, I wonder if I should have just stayed where I'd come back to life and waited. Maybe someone had provoked me to wake up and was coming back to get me; maybe it was a coincidence that magic failed and I woke up. I give myself a slap. That type of doubtful and distracted thinking is not going to help me.

I push open the door of the tavern and step in. It's dusty and poorly lit, with perhaps ten patrons inside. They aren't dressed like the people outside who wore the simplest of farmer clothes. These all seem to have their own style and personality, though they all need a wash. Maybe they're wanderers like me.

An old guy with a grizzled face gives me a scowl from a table about six feet away. Two women in dirty brown cloaks are playing cards on the other side of the room. They stop to give me a glare. One of them has dark hair and a pained look on her face. A group of six put their glasses down in unison and look at me, but they don't flinch or say a thing. Weird group of customers. Licking my lips in the silence, I realize that when I opened the door, there wasn't a single person talking. The hair on the best of my neck, as soaked and filthy as it is, stands up.

I lift my gaze to check out the ceiling. It's all exposed wood beams, some of which are sagging badly. Sunlight's poking through the sorry roof in several places. The building's definitely seen better days, but I'm willing to bet it's not going to come down anytime soon.

With my pistol pointed at the floor and my other hand innocently at my side, I slowly make my way up to the bar at the far end. Sighing, I rest my arms on its dingy, black railing, my pistol still firmly in hand.

On the wooden shelves behind the bar are mostly broken and empty bottles. A few here and there show hopeful signs of having some type of liquid comfort. Good thing I'm not fussy.

I catch a glimpse of someone moving behind the bar at the other end, and watch without turning my head. It's a woman, wearing a brown and grey dress.

"Are you looking to cause trouble?" she asks, leaning against the bar.

I raise an eyebrow, as it seems a weird thing to say. Turning to look at her, I lose my words for a minute. Half of her face appears to be covered in black ash or paint. On the light side she's got a bright, brown eye that's glaring at me, on the other side I'm not even sure there's an eye. Her long hair's a filthy, matted black.

Without thinking, I take a half-step back. Everyone in the room twitches and I say in a slow and easy voice, "No. I'd just like to get a drink; maybe have a bite to eat. Then go." I nod at the bottles. "Looks like you might have something."

She nods at my pistol and then locks her gaze on me. "You can't have weapons like that in here. Bringing them into our town uninvited is asking for trouble,". Her voice is wrong somehow. She doesn't sound like a bartender, more like someone pretending to be one. I glance over my shoulder at the patrons, no one's moved. They're all just looking at me. Scratching my cheek, I stare down at the railing. My guts are churning, but it's nothing to do with magic or mana. Tapping my free hand's fingers on the bar, I bite my lip while I find my words.

"It's a scary world out there," I reply. "I've been traveling for a while and came upon your village. Like I said, I'd like something to eat and drink, and then I'll be happy to go on my way." I rub my temple trying to get rid of images of crazed religious types who might want to sacrifice me to their pretend gods. There's a memory rumbling around having to do with something like that.

She does a weird sideways head motion that unnerves me. "You're going to have to hang the pistol on the wall there by the front door. The sword you can give to me." She puts her hand out, the one from the light side. I notice the other one's curled up and tucked into her chest. Staring at her face, I'm not sure it's pain she's feeling. It's almost like she's concentrating. Looking her up and down, I'm pretty sure she's nothing like Ania, but something's definitely not right with her.

There's no smile or emotion in her face. My vision wanders, looking for where the door that's not the front door could be, because otherwise she wouldn't have said it like that. It never hurts to know where the exits are, especially when you're considering blowing the whole situation up. Tilting my head down, I sneak a peek back at the patrons. This time I catch the glint of a blade from one of the cloaked women. There's a barrel showing itself from beneath the old man's folded hands. Looks like they're thinking of taking it to the next level too.

As I turn my back to lean on the railing, I see we've got extra company. Over a dozen the folks from outside are now gathered at the front door. I lick my lips and nod my bowed head as I reply. "Sorry, lady, I can't do that."

episode fifteen

The bartender takes a step backwards, her open hand disappearing below the bar. "Then we've got a problem," she says, her voice a bit stilted and with a real edge to it.

I run my free hand along the cold, metal railing and sigh nice and loud. My other hand has an iron grip on my pistol which she's eyeing intently.

The creaking of old knees and the skidding of chairs behind me confirms that my time's just about run out. Sweat drips from my forehead, and runs down my back. My mouth's dry and my mood's eroding like a sandy cliff in a hurricane.

The only thing holding me back is knowing how stiff and sloppy this body is, and not being able to count on it. At least I'm shooting better than I remember. But against this group, I'm not sure I'm getting out without some kind of help. A small part of me wonders if I should just surrender my weapons, but the rest does its best to pound those thoughts into the back of my mind.

Staring up at the bottles on the shelf, it dawns on me that I don't even have a way to pay. Way to go, smart guy. You come waltzing in, stirring up trouble, and even if they agreed, you've got nothing. I need to stop being an idiot.

I turn to the bartender again, a forced smile on my face. The dark side of her face is even more unnerving now that I'm looking at it dead on. It's wrinkled and leathery, like it's from an eighty-year-old woman who's spent her life in the sun. But the other half looks like that of a reasonably attractive woman in her twenties, maybe thirties.

"Last chance to—" she stops herself and starts sniffing the air like a dog. Her one good eye is closed and her head is moving left and right. I resist the urge to pull back as she comes right up close to me. At first it seems funny, then weird, but when she opens her eye, a memory cracks through. "Yigging leecher!" I yell. As I move to step back, she leaps at me, grabbing my pistol arm.

In a heartbeat, the world falls away.

Shaking my head, I give myself a good slap. I can't afford to fall asleep, not when there are Scourge Patrols about. A shiver goes down my spine as I think of those elite squads of soldiers, each led by a ruthless, devoted acolyte. While the will of soldiers may waiver, even with their enchanted armor and weapons, an acolyte will rarely ever deviate from the orders of the ruling Wizard or their delegates. The last thing I need is to be asleep when they show up, and they will. I can't avoid them forever.

Waving the smoke from the putrid-smelling campfire out of my face, I pull the raggedy furs up and tighter. It's cold, and the wind's whistling in the background.

Looking up, I'm confused by the complete lack of stars. Feeling something in my hands, I find a dirty, wooden bowl. It's empty of its vile contents, which I can still feel slithering down to my stomach. The taste is still lingering, as is the appreciation for having had a meal.

Squinting at the others sitting around the fire, I feel I know them. It's weird. Closing my eyes and concentrating, I'm certain I've been here before. Opening my eyes, I glance about. Wasn't there a leecher? I rub the back of my neck. I must be losing my mind. This feels right. Maybe I'd nodded off, had a bad dream for a minute. I can't shake the sense that this is all so familiar, it's almost a memory. The leecher thing feels further and further away with every passing second.

The shadowy forms are huddled together for warmth and protection. They aren't taking any particular note of me, leaving me to my less than social ways. We've been hiding for days, moving every two nights or so. They're risking their lives to protect me, all because I showed them the Scourge Patrols aren't immortal like they pretend to be.

Rubbing the middle of my forehead, I think back to a week ago. I was passing through a market here in the under-city of Banareal. Only the poor and ruthless opportunists live in the shadow of the great floating behemoth that is Banareal. It's cold and little grows. They say that benefits trickle down from the top of the ruling Wizard's tower where he stays, down to the people, but like so many things, it's fiction meant to pacify the masses.

Scratching my stubbly face, I can't remember why they were hunting me. I remember killing the acolyte, that arrogant yig. The Scourge soldiers were already laying waste to the market before that, but after, they went completely crazy. Hiding behind their painted masks, they unleashed the worst of themselves. And with the acolyte killed before their very eyes, the people had risen up with me. It was horrible but just, to see the soldiers ripped apart. For every person the soldiers killed, there were ten more to take their place. Before other Scourge Patrols showed up, I was ushered away.

With a heavy sigh, I glance around at the people again. I have a horrible feeling that their kindness is going to be rudely rewarded, but I don't know why.

I reach down and touch the ground. I don't expect it to be firm, flat and dusty. Craning my head and squinting into the dark, I realize we're inside an abandoned building, likely in the basement.

Around the campfire I hear the worried voices of children asking the same questions they've asked for days, and tired parents who are losing faith in their answers.

Putting my hands out to warm them, I'm surprised to see my tattoos. Why am I surprised? I've always had them.

I stand up and put my back to the fire, staring into the inky darkness, waiting. Something's supposed to happen. Something's coming and it should be here any minute. Maybe this is a memory?

A glint of light shows up in the distance, and then wavers, it's beam becoming wider until it's pointed straight at us. They've found us.

"Scourge!" I yell to the group, but it doesn't help. By the time anyone understands what's going on, I'm sent flying into a column.

This Scourge's acolyte isn't a rookie. He issues his commands quickly and clearly, and then moves as a blur of blue and silver.

My world's spinning. If I had any weapons, they're gone. There's a boot keeping my head down and a blade touching my back. The taste of blood and dirt helps keep me awake. I gaze out helplessly at the slummers.

One by one, they're cut down, until only a mother and little daughter are left. I remember having watched the mother run her finger along the inside of her dinner bowl and hold it out for the girl to lick.

As the daughter is pulled away, the mother throws a soldier to the ground. Despite her petite frame and lack of formal training, she puts up a good fight until three of them are on her. The acolyte laughs and takes an interest. My stomach turns as I suspect what's coming. I'm tempted to look away, but I can't, it feels like I'd be abandoning her. I try to stand but the boot and blade remind me that I'm not going anywhere.

The acolyte waves away the soldier who is holding the daughter. The kid wisely just stands there. Some points of light circle around her. Probably floating lanterns.

With a sharp gesture and whispered word, the acolyte forces the girl to her knees, and with another, makes her lean forward, head out. The acolyte is so wasteful with his mana, I can feel the residue on my face from here.

He walks over to the girl, paralyzed with fear and held in place by his will, and raises a hand above her neck. I remember the first time I'd seen an acolyte behead someone with their hand, it'd sent a bolt of fear through me. They love doing this to the stunted. Yes, that's what they're called. Those who can't touch the world of magic and mana. There are the Wizards, the acolytes, the adepts, the wesleks, and the stunted.

I've heard a million screams, but never one like the one that which erupts out of this mother. It's the scream of the powerless trying to shake something loose in the universe, trying to shock Fate into giving them a chance.

Her face contorts and her body twists. She manages to knock one of the soldiers backwards, and then to my surprise, she sends another flying one several feet. Limply, the woman hobbles forward. I notice the shadow of only one arm at her side, and as she comes into the light, I see the other one's curled up to her chest. She bends down and grabs a stone.

"What did you just do?" asks the acolyte, speaking for the two of us. I can tell by the look on his face that she didn't just throw those soldiers, she must have done something else to them.

The mother pulls her arm back and when she lets the stone go, there's a boom. The acolyte falls forward, light shining through a fist-sized hole through his chest. The daughter collapses to the ground in tears.

The mother clumsily dashes for her daughter and then skids to a stop, resting on all fours. Half of her body seems dark, and only one eye's shining in the light. Her nose is raised in the air. What's she doing? The soldiers don't know what to make of her or the death of their leader. She turns about, sniffing and then glares hungrily at a particular soldier. I can tell by his uniform that he's an adept, able to enhance his skills with mana. It's a massacre. I barely get out of there, the only one alive.

"Leecher…" I whisper as I pass out and the world slips away.

My head hits the floor with a wallop. The leecher bartender leaps over the bar, kicking me accidentally on her way towards the door. She's yelling something, but I can't make sense of it.

Staring at the ceiling, I feel weak and drained. What could have made her leave? Then I hear the screech of the carnu. Yig, they've tracked me down.

All I can manage is to roll my head a bit to the left and right. Spit's riding down the side of my face, and my arms and legs are jelly. The only thing I can feel is my heart pounding so hard I can barely breathe.

The sounds of battle are drawing closer, though it's strange. The only actual voices I hear are that of the leecher and the carnu, no one else.

At one point, one of the carnu screams in pain, and I immediately remember an image of a Wizard's laboratory, and tables upon tables of strapped down stunted being experimented on. "They're made... yig, they're experiments... I was there when they made the first one." I'm surprised by my own words. Narrowing my eyes, I focus in on the memory as much as I can. My heart skips a beat and I glance about frantically, muttering the truth I finally can grasp, "They were made to hunt and kill rogue wesleks, adepts, and acolytes. Yig me." I force my body to turn so I can stare at the door. "He's coming and nothing's going to stop him." Gritting my teeth, I force my head up and try to get my upper body to follow suit. "Come on."

In the doorway are two silhouettes, probably what's left of the original patrons. Outside, I hear one of the carnu roar and a loud whooshing sound. Whimpers follow.

I've only got sensitivity in one finger. Carefully, so as not to get the attention of the patrons who are preparing themselves for the inevitable, I run my finger over my body until I find my short sword. "Oh Mother of Mercy, thank you for still being there," I mutter. Taking hold of it, I wait. Nothing happens. Blinking desperately, I think about touching the etched markings at the base of the blade again. Taking in a big breath, I get my head up again and watch as my clumsy fingers finally get the job done. With a sigh, I take some healing and pull all the remaining mana out of it, which isn't much.

As I roll over on to my chest, my body now only feeling like I've been in a bad bar fight, I hear the wood crunch at the doorway. Glancing up, I swallow hard. The scarred carn is staring past the two patrons and right at me.

episode sixteen

One of the silhouettes raises his pistol at the scarred carn. It reaches out with its muscular clawed arm and takes hold of him. The old man struggles and then goes up in flames in the carn's iron grip. The doorway and wall catch fire while he burns. Giving the smoldering corpse a shake for good measure, the carn then throws the remains into the corner.

As the other patron backs away, I realize it's one of the cloaked women from the card game. She's holding two long, serrated blades in her hands and is shifting her weight back and forth trying to find an opening.

The carn shifts its attention to her and takes two more steps into the bar. Pushing its shoulders down, I watch in disbelief as its mage-head rises up on a black and spiny tendril. Panic runs rampant through me, and I start shaking my hands and feet violently to get them to wake the yig up!

The mage-head moves like a serpent, floating three feet from the body, which is taking steps to counter each one taken by the woman.

When the yig did carn get the ability to do that? Why didn't it do that before? I glance about. It must be the confined space. Yig me. "Come on, get up!" I tell my fumbling body as I try to get everything in place to stand.

The carn starts emitting a disturbing clicking sound from its chest. It's out of synch with the movements of the skull. It's dizzying, making it hard to think. I focus on the floor and try to block it out. Out of the corner of my eye, I notice a shadow growing behind the carn. A nervous chuckle escapes me as I try to imagine who would be so foolish as to approach a carn.

Finally, I get myself up to a kneeling position, thankful that the carn hasn't taken notice yet. I see my pistol several feet away, on the floor under a chair. Even if I could get to it, I don't know if I have enough mana to do anything. I know I've got some from my sword, but I don't feel anything inside.

The woman slashes at the carn's head, missing. Another swipe gets it to back up a few steps into the doorway. At first, I'm shaking my head at how badly she missed, then I realize that wasn't what she was trying to accomplish. Dozens of arms grab on to a part of the scarred carn from behind, despite its flames, and haul it out of the bar.

Without a thought, I snatch my short sword off the floor and stand, pointing it at the woman. "Are we going to have a problem?"

She stares at me with white eyes and an expressionless face. "Oh freaking yig, oners." My stomach sinks as I finally realize she's connected to the arms and probably all the other people I've seen so far. I step back slowly, hoping that the hive-mind is more focused on taking on the two carnu than me.

Her head turns as I move. "I'm getting out of here," I tell her, slip my sword away and scoop up my pistol, my eyes on her the whole time. As I take a step, she points her two black, serrated swords at me.

Staring at her face, I remember something about oners being an infection, taking over the living hosts. They're alive, just the will and sense of self is suppressed. I glance at her hands, which are thankfully covered in dark leather gloves. She's not looking to make me one of them.

All of a sudden I feel magic drop hard and fast. She stumbles and falls over, while I drop to my knees and throw up. Shaking my head, I force myself to my feet. She's looking lost. She jerks her head about, strangely. Maybe they use magic to communicate? Huh, interesting, but a thought for another day.

A loud whoosh grabs my attention. The entire ceiling and the beams are ablaze. "I've got to get out of here." Scanning about, I can't see Randmon. "Randmon, if you're here, get out!"

There's a roar at the doorway and my shoulders slump. I don't need to look back to know the carn's standing there. Even still, I can't help myself and glance over my shoulder. The scarred carn's standing there, bloody and with dark spots on its body, some of them large. I don't think anything can stop it.

I fall on the floor, a sense of vertigo as my stomach tells me that magic's rocketing back. Propping myself up with one arm, I aim my pistol squarely at the carn's black scar. "Want some more?"

Staring into the mage-skull's eyes, a memory breaks through. I'm twelve years old and strapped to a table, someone looking over me. Words I heard a thousand times ring in my ears: *Great wesleks are made, not found.* The Old Man, he helped me escape. He was the first of us. The carn and I stare at each other, one magical experiment to another.

Bouncing my leg nervously, I keep darting my eyes back and forth between the carn and the oner woman, who's got her blades back in hand. The three of us stand there, waiting. Suddenly the carn flinches, screams, and falls to its knees.

The hair on the back of my neck stands up as the carn looks at me in pain. A sense of fear and a yearning for help washes over me. I shake my head to clear it.

The carn tries to reach around its back, but can't

and then it falls forward, it's flames barely visible.

I reaffirm my sweaty grip on my pistol and swipe a hand across my soaked upper lip as I stare at the shadow behind it. What the yig can bring down a carn like that?

Stepping into the bar, I see it's the leecher, her eyes wild. The once-dark side of her face looks fine, almost sparkling.

"Yigging Mother of Mercy, what the—?" My arm starts to tremble as I push myself backwards. If she drained the carn, I can't imagine what she'll be able to do now. Leechers are untrained and unpredictable.

The oner woman takes a step back and then drops her hands at her side. I flip my gaze between the two of them, something's not making sense. I've never heard of oners having an alliance with anyone, and leechers are always consumed by their addiction to mana.

The leecher plants her hands back on the carn and it moans, another wave of emotion washing over me. It's mage-skull lies there, a foot away from the rest of the body, attached by the tendril. I feel like it's looking at me.

I'm tempted to touch the oner to see if I can drain her, given that she's supposed to be alive, but for all I know I'd bring the infection along too. Involuntary suicide isn't the plan, and I don't know what I can safely drain or not. Is it people? Or was that guy I killed a weslek like me and I just pulled his mana too fast?

The leecher lets go of the carn and stands, staring straight at me. "Thanks for inviting your friends."

"No friends of mine," I reply. The fire's spreading to everything, last will be the wall behind the bar. Gazing up, I notice the big beams are well on their way. I think I've been in worse situations, but I was a different person then, and this version of me is a sweaty, heart-pounding mess.

I straighten and raise my pistol arm, but she sees it coming a mile away. She's a blur that sends me crashing over the bar into the shelves and bottles.

Groaning, I hastily right myself and search desperately for my pistol, quickly finding it. I catch a glimpse of Randmon and snatch him up too. "We're getting out of here," I say, placing him on my shoulder.

With a short, steadying breath, I peer over the bar. The leecher's staring at the floor, her face tight in concentration. The oner woman looks like a statue.

The carn's starting to stir, its mage-skull tendril slowly pulling back into its neck. Yig, he's a tough beast. The leecher has her back to him. In the distance, I hear the other carn calling out. It's coming quickly.

Biting my lip, I swiftly change my target to the

drained carn. Just as it looks at me, I pull the trigger. My pistol fizzles, and I see in its eyes that I've truly made an enemy for life. Another idiot move. I can only hope that the scarred carn's ticked off enough with the leecher to go for her before hunting me down.

Using the bar for cover, I make my way towards the end until I catching a glimpse of light. I don't see an actual door, but I throw all my weight in that direction and find myself outside the burning tavern.

Stumbling into the grassy area behind the burning building, I fall on the ground and laugh nervously. There is a sound like thunder. I glance up at the sky, but that's not it. Turning, my sense of relief instantly evaporates as I see dozens of oners running full tilt towards the burning bar, and me.

episode seventeen

The landscape is flooded with oners of all colors, creeds, ages and sizes. They move in disturbing unison, independently and collaboratively, helping the fallen up. They all have the same intense look on their white-eyed faces, and the same tattered clothes.

I run as fast as I can but there's nowhere to go. As the human river races around me, I'm elbowed, shouldered, kneed, and shoved mercilessly. Screaming at them is pointless, a whisper against their thunderous footfalls. As the wounds pile up, I find myself repeating the mantra: "Stay standing, stay alive." The memory of seeing a man fall in a riot once flashes by, the horror reinforcing my resolve.

The sea of white eyes glance at me as they sail onwards to surround the bar. I can tell I'm logged in their collective mind, and once they're done with the carn, they're coming for me.

As the last oner passes, I'm shoved from behind and land face first in the once pristine grass, now pulpy mud. Every joint, every muscle and fiber of my being is in agony. Of all places to die, I don't want it to be here in the mud.

A shadow appears over me. I wonder if there's a oner who's been assigned to keep an eye on me. Coughing, I try to summon the strength to get up, but rolling over is as far as I get. I lazily watch the blazing bar and the swarm of oners around it, some on the shoulders or backs of others. The bar sways back and forth and finally comes down in a fiery crash.

Despite my desperate wishes, my limbs refuse to do my bidding. What's going on? With each blink, my eyes are taking more and more energy to force open, and stay open for less time. My breathing's getting heavier. Come on, got to get up. I start to move, surprised to see my hand locked in a death-grip around my pistol. Maybe I need to rest just a minute.

"Hey, weslek, you've been staring at that pistol for a while. Is that what you want or is there something else?"

I turn to look at the steely-faced woman leaning against a white, stone counter. Her arms are folded and she seems at home. She's wearing a red jerkin with green sleeves, and black pants. Her long, red hair is done up in a bun, with a strand dangling down over one shoulder. She has an intricately designed, empty leather holster under one arm and another like it on her hip.

"You're the... the smith."

She squints at me. "What's going on? Are you feeling okay?" She comes right up to, inspecting my face. "You seem a little off. You didn't look like this when you walked in here a minute ago."

Taking a step backwards, I wave a hand. "Sorry, I'm just having a bad day. Things have been intense lately. I guess it's starting to catch up with me."

Glancing about, I take in the room. The walls are dark wood, with sections decorated with beautiful firearms, from small pistols to rifles. There are several bright, gas-powered lanterns hanging from the exposed ceiling, leaving few shadows. There are a few swords of various types, here and there, for additional decor.

She returns to leaning against the counter. I follow her gaze and find I'm cradling a pistol in my hands. It's silver with an etched floral design. There's a deep, rich, blue line that runs from the hilt to the tip. "Huh."

"Is huh good?" she asks.

I bring it up for a closer inspection but shake my head. "I can't place it, but it looks familiar."

She scoffs. "No one comes into my workshop without me being here, I remember faces, and I've not seen yours. I've designed every one of these myself, and I'm sure you haven't seen that before. Do you know how hard it was to get the quality of crushed sapphires I needed to create the mana channel? Never mind the level of expertise it took to make it work? That pistol is my greatest work of art."

"It's beautiful," I offer, glancing up with a half-hearted smile. Holding it in one hand, I point it at the wall and try to imagine myself using it. Part of the hilt digs into one of my knuckles. "The weight feels right, but the grip's awkward."

"You sound disappointed, but the grip wasn't designed for you. It's easy enough to change if that's what you want. I'll need a cast of your hand and about three days to do it. Your buddy already gave me enough coin to cover whatever you want, so make it count." She pushed a sleeve back and glanced at an ebony rectangle affixed to her forearm. "Better make it quick, apparently there's a Scourge being released in this district." Looking me over quickly, she bites her lip, stopping herself from asking the obvious.

"What is that?" I ask, curious.

"None of your business," she says, covering it back up.

My knees suddenly go weak, but I catch myself. I lean against the wall, shaking my head, trying to clear the cobwebs.

"Don't you dare be sick in here," she snaps. I notice a sleek piece of black steel peeking out from the edge of her pants. She's keeping it tucked almost out of sight, wanting me to see it but wanting me to know that she doesn't consider me an outright threat just yet. I've used that technique many times. I'm curious what it is, but don't dare ask.

"Just a bit light-headed," I tell her. "That's all. I like this one. Can you modify it to have a longer barrel? I like more control. Also, no flowery stuff on the grip... if you don't mind. It'd like it sleek and flat."

"Flat?"

"In case I need to strap it against the bottom of something. Flat doesn't stick out as much."

"Strapped to something like, I don't know, a levi-car?" She straightens up. "You're aiming to pass through a checkpoint, get to the under-city." She narrows her eyes at me. "You don't have a permit to leave, do you?"

I stare at the ground and shrug, then look back up at her. "You don't want to know, do you?"

"No, I don't," she replies. The black steel disappears, likely into a holster on the back of her leg. Her expression's steely, but her eyes show concern. She grabs my head with both hands before I can react. "Did you get slammed on the way in?"

"Slammed?" I ask, squinting. It feels like my thoughts are traipsing through molasses. "I can't... I know that word, don't I?" Suddenly I'm struck with a sense of panic. My eyes dart about, her grip firm on my head. "Where's Randmon?"

"Who? There's been no one else here but you and me since you got here." She rubs her thumbs along my cheeks and then lets my head go.

Scratching my beard, I'm not sure either.

She inspects her thumbs. "No mana residue. Hmm…" She strokes her forehead with an index finger; her eyes locked on mine. "Do the words slammed, bolted, spelled… any of this ringing a bell?"

I shrug, lowering my gaze. "It's getting harder to think."

"They're common Banareali slang." She gives me an unsettling stare, the type that threatens to peel the stain off wood. "I need to check something." Putting a hand in the air, she murmurs, her eyes glowing bright green for a moment. "Nothing, that's… disappointing. Why are you frowning?"

"I didn't hear you do that in my head."

She glares at me while she straightens her jerkin. "Well, you're no Wizard. And unless you're secretly a weslek, in which case I'd have to shoot you right here and now, because there's no way I'm letting a Scourge come in here and destroy my life, the only reason you'd expect to hear voices in your head would be because you're extra special crazy. I'm not keen on that, no matter the money I got paid upfront."

I drop my gaze to the floor, wondering what she knows. I'm tempted to ask. There's no sense of memories lingering around in my mind, as if the lake that was me has dried up, or I'm simply in the wrong place. I massage my chest, right over my heart, wincing in unexpected pain. Then my legs give out. She catches me, sliding me down to the ground. Her expression is three different flavors of frustrated. I'm running out of time, and she's running out of patience.

She pulls a stool out from a closet I didn't even realize was there, and helps me up. "I don't talk to people on the floor, not in my shop."

After perching me on it, I watch as her shoulders rise and her head moves back. "You should go." She points to the grand door. It's intricately carved, six feet wide, and only a few feet away. Oddly, it takes me two attempts to see it. Weird.

"No, I'm okay." I lean against the wall, hanging my head. "I came to ask you about making a pistol, right?"

Her nostrils flare, and she snatches the pistol out of my hands.

I stare down at my hand that was holding it. Flexing my fingers, I can't understand why my hand feels full, why my arm still feels heavy.

"It's hard to think. I'm just making sure that I'm saying everything, not leaving any bits in my head."

She pulls up her sleeve and glances at the ebony rectangle again. "You've got five minutes before I have to throw you out."

"I like that one." I point to the pistol in her hands.

"Really? Buying it for a Wizard or someone?"

I raise an eyebrow.

She closes her eyes and shakes her head, withdrawing the question. "It gives you the best of both worlds."

My face contorts as I fight to concentrate. There's an excruciating pain in my stomach. "The... the both part... where?" I'm blinking hard. Yig, it's like I'm fighting for every single thought. "Where?"

Keeping her sharp eyes trained on me, she turns the pistol over. "Right here at the bottom of the grip, this switch flips it. You reload the gunpowder bullets by—"

I start to fall forward.

"Woo! Hey, stay with me. Stay..."

Everything's black. There's nothing, just a familiar, twisting sensation somewhere... My thoughts are like a cloud being dispersed by a ferocious wind.

There's a moment of heat. It comes again, but this time, I recognize it. My thoughts coalesce around it.

It's pain. The third time, I realize that I exist. I'm a thing, and someone's hitting me. "Grrr..." I force my eyes open to the thinnest of slits.

The blazing light of day is raw agony. I'm face down in the muck... I fight to move; my muscles consider but then refuse my demand. In the distance, I see orange and red, and a blurry mass. I blink again and again, trying to focus. The glint of the sun on steel catches my eye, and I see my hand's still clasping the pistol, my pistol.

There's a shadow over top of me, moving. It strikes me again, screaming, "GIVE ME THE REST OF IT!"

Randmon's head pokes out of a hole, and a single, clear thought takes hold of my mind: I've got seconds before I'm dead.

Spotting a stone embedded in the mud, I rally every scrap of my being and smack the pistol's handle on it. I quickly point the pistol behind me and fumble my numb fingers until I hear the deafening boom. As I'm sprayed with wetness, my wrist, elbow and shoulder erupt in such horrific anguish that the world vanishes from me.

episode eighteen

A deep rumble, like distant thunder, rouses me out of my dreamless sleep. I lay there, skipping off the oblivion of unconsciousness. Wood creaks nearby, getting my attention. I open my bleary eyes the thinnest of slits to investigate.

The room's agonizingly bright. There's a figure moving about near me. After blinking a few times to clear up my vision, I let my eyes wander. The rafters look like the type I'd find in a house. For some reason, I can't turn my head. At the edge of my vision it seems like there's a window with ratty curtains. I'm guessing it's afternoon.

I can't feel anything, it's weird. I can't even tell if I've got a body beyond my chest. My arms, legs, fingers... it's like they don't exist. Whoever or whatever the silhouette is, it didn't kill me for a reason. I just have to figure out what that reason is.

I close my eyes and think. For ages, I concentrate on moving one finger. There's something... it's rough and worn. It's exhausting but I keep at it. It's wood.

The floor must be wood, not dirt. I'm lying on a wooden floor. A fragile little smile cracks free.

Glancing at the silhouette, I decide to take a leap of faith and let myself fall asleep.

When I wake up, every muscle hurts and feels tight like I haven't moved in ages. Taking a full breath, I open my eyes, willing myself to accept my new state over the last one. I'm relieved to find my head willing to move about on command.

The silhouette's a cloaked figure, standing near one of the three windows. The place is barren, except for a large wooden table several feet away and what looks like wooden kitchen cabinets without the doors. It's hard to tell from here, but they look empty.

The cloaked figure walks from one window to the next. A sheath's poking out from under the cloak… no, two. Okay, so this person's pretty serious.

"Hey…" I whisper, my tongue flopping about in my mouth like a fat piece of meat.

The shadowy form doesn't turn, instead moves to the next window. "You're awake, good. Can you move? We won't be safe here for much longer." The voice is definitively female, but her tempo is strange, stilted.

"Barely…" I reply.

The figure comes over and crouches down beside me. Her cloak's dark grey, and she's got black leather boots, both of which are caked with beige dust and blood. The hand closest to me is gloved in dark leather. Her face is hidden beneath the hood, almost as if she were a figment.

"Who are you? Why did you save me?" I ask.

She pulls back the hood. At first I notice her shoulder-length, black hair but then my heart skips a beat as I see her eyes; they're white. Just what type of twisted mess have I gotten myself into? "You're the oner from the bar."

She glances away, and after a few seconds, nods.

"Why did you save me?"

Pulling her glove off, she puts a hand on my forehead. I try to resist but I'm barely able to squirm before she's pulled her hand back and put the glove back on.

"There's nothing to fear. I'm glad to see that you have recovered. Our... healer said you should recover. We used their knowledge until they died... the carn..." She stands up and looks away.

"I'm sorry," I say, this time my tongue cooperating better. "So you lose knowledge when one of you die?"

"Elements of them remain, but most of what they know fades."

I roll my head around, enjoying the cracking it makes. "I thought when someone became an oner, the hive—"

Shivering at the term, she walks back to the first window. "We are an aggregate, a commune. There is no hive."

Clumsily, I move my arm, trying to get my hand to my face. It reminds me of when I've slept on it. I can barely feel that it's there, just barely. "Why am I still breathing? Why are you protecting me? Or are you?"

This time, I notice the bizarre way she nods. It's like my question hangs there in the air while she considers it, and then she moves her head back and waits, before committing to the nod. It sends a shiver down my spine. In that off-tempo voice of hers, she says, "You had a choice to shoot the carn or this One, and you chose the carn."

"It didn't do any good," I reply.

She frowns. "You made the choice, and it got our attention. Then you..." she stiffens, then bows her head slightly. "You freed us by killing the Second."

I force myself to roll over onto my forearms, a satisfied smile on my face afterwards. Bit by bit, my body's waking up but everything's dragging. Resting my head on the floor, I ask, "What's a Second? Never heard of that. Does it have to do with the bartender? The leecher?"

"Yes..." I hear her step back and forth before continuing. "She came with another woman weeks ago. We allowed them to stay, preferring to work on the land as long as they did not interfere with our colony. The village was deserted before us, so there wasn't an issue with space."

Stifling a laugh, I shake my head at just how wrong all the academics in the world are. My memories were still a mess, but I knew enough to know that no one had any idea that oners could work peacefully in groups. Then, as I lift my head up, a suspicious thought dawns on me. What if she's playing me? I glance about for Randmon, curious what his take on everything is. Squinting, I'm pretty sure I see his little nose peeking out from behind one of the table legs. Little guy's probably hungry. That's when I realize just how starved and parched I am.

"Hey, do you have anything to eat?"

"Your inner body likely isn't functioning properly yet, you should wait."

Raising an eyebrow, I nod. "I hadn't thought about that. So what's this Second business?"

"The second woman grabbed an oner, trying to get our blessing and when denied, revealed she and the other were leechers. She started draining that One. The other woman then drained the first, and in doing so, gained a connection to our colony. When she exerted her magic, she could overwhelm our will, and became the second voice. Thus she is called the

Second."

Shaking my head, I fumble my hand to my face and scratch it. I notice my beard's gone, but ignore it. "Wow. I've never heard of that."

"Neither had we," she says, shrugging, a hint of sadness in her voice.

Pushing myself backwards onto my legs, I take a moment to breathe and go through what she's said. "When she drained the carn, what did that do? Boost her?"

"We've only ever had a colony of up to a dozen, but with her, she could pull others in. With the carn's mana, she was able to pull in the surrounding colonies. It was overwhelming for some of the others, their minds couldn't take it."

"They died?"

She nods, her fists clenched.

"Why didn't you?"

"This One was an adept before receiving the blessing. It was painful, but we managed to resist it."

I rub my stubbly chin. "So it was her that I shot behind me?"

"Yes," she replies quickly.

"And when I killed her... you got your own mind back?"

She stares at me, with those unnerving white eyes. "Yes."

"What happened to the carn?" I ask.

Lowering her gaze to the floor, another shiver runs down my spine. "It is the reason we aren't safe. It has been hunting for you."

My blood runs cold. "Are there any of you outside?"

"A few."

"There were hundreds, and now there are only a few?"

She raises a finger, her head moving about as if trying to hear the others. "There are only four of us now."

"Yig me," I say, wiping my face with both hands. "How the yig could the carn survive? How did you survive?"

"This One helped kill the other carn, but the scarred one... it wouldn't stop. We might have won, if we hadn't kept losing our way."

I squint as I try to make sense of it all. "Losing your way... do you mean when magic stops?"

She nods.

My eyebrows go up as my mind runs through the likely scene. "That must have been a slaughter."

Her face is eerily expressionless. She gazes at the floor, just blinking. "There were hundreds of us at first. Many colonies, fighting as one."

I pause for a second, something not making sense.

Unable to place my finger on it, I decide to try and stand. Planting one foot and pushing off my knee, I stumble about like a drunk idiot. She watches as I slam into a wall and fall back to the floor. "I'm okay."

Her brow furrows for a moment. "I know," she replies, unconcerned. "We are one less now... The carn is heading in our direction. Hopefully the other two can lead it away."

"Where are we?"

"This is our southern feeding house. When we work these fields, we bring our food here to prepare and eat together."

I look down at the floor and notice how there's a well-worn path from the front door and around the table. I can only imagine a dozen oners walking in with baskets and whatever, preparing and eating a meal in silence together. It's unnerving, and yet another thing no one's going to believe if I ever get the chance to tell them.

Closing my eyes, I rack my brain for what could be going on, and then it hits me. "You think I can do something to help you; that's why I'm here, isn't it?"

For a split second, her face isn't dispassionate or detached. It's difficult for me to tell if it's fear or what, but there's something. I wait patiently for her to answer me.

She blinks for a few seconds, her face once again

passive. "The leecher's attack should have killed you, but didn't. You're incredibly strong, useful. There's very little left for us here now. Our neighbors are damaged too. We need to leave. We need your help." Her expression's subtle, but there's truth to what she's saying.

I sit up and shake my head. "I don't know what to tell you, but I can't do much. I'm not a Wizard, or even an adept... I can fight, somewhat, but that's about all I can do." Eyeing her carefully, I watch for... something. Something that can explain why my gut's telling me there's something more to the story. Part of me thinks this is all in my head, and that the strange vibe I'm getting from her is just because she's a oner. All the weird pauses and moments where she looks like a statue for a few seconds really throws me off.

"You can help us get to safety. We need to get moving."

With a big breath, I stand and spread my arms out like a kid walking on a log. Glancing at her, I'd swear I see the very edge of her mouth turn up. "Okay, if I'm going to help, I'm going to need my short sword and pistol."

She stares at me, her fists clenching for a moment before replying, her speech extra-stilted this time for some reason, "They are in a sack, slung on this One's back under the cloak. Given your condition, we believe it best that we hold on to them for now."

"Fair enough," I lie. Nothing says you don't trust a man more than not giving him his weapons back. But I don't have any choice, so I smile.

She drops her gaze to the floor, her eyes close.

"What happened?"

"They are gone," she replies.

I rub my forehead, trying to make sense of her clenched fists and blank face. "You mean the other oners?"

She nods. "We must move, the carn is coming."

My eyes dart about, my fingers twitching as I think up a plan. "Is there a stable around here? Maybe some animals we could ride or something?"

The oner shakes her head. "The only thing is an old levi-car, but it won't work. We had a mechanic One once, he said it lacked life."

"Life? Yig, get me to it. Take me there, now!"

She grabs my arm and puts it around her neck. Opening the front door, my heart sinks as we see a golden field of wheat ablaze on the opposite side of the road. I don't remember the wheat being so high, but it doesn't matter. I swallow hard and put everything I can into moving.

episode nineteen

Sticking to the southern edge of the road, we hurry as the inferno on the other side roars. After a few minutes, I dare to let go and start jogging on my own. There's nothing like fear to boost one's eagerness to get the body moving properly. My mind keeps ignoring the wheat field on the southern side that's just waiting to burst into flame, I'm sure. I stare in fear at each and every fiery ember that dances on the breeze.

The road snakes back and forth and finally dips, revealing a rust-roofed barn half a mile away in a valley. "Geez, do you guys plant crops everywhere?" I mutter, hoping for a scarred landscape that would give us some refuge.

"Yes, to do otherwise would be wasteful."

I raise an eyebrow at her as she runs ahead. I can't buy that oners are simply communities of people working for a common good. There's got to be something going on. I stop in my tracks and glance about; thankfully there's nothing. Paranoid, I close my eyes to see if I can hear any voices or anything, in case she gave me their blessing or whatever it is. Nothing. Wait, there's something else though. "Hey! Hey, oner! Stop!"

She slides to a stop. "What are you doing?"

"It's like I can feel it," I say, rubbing my hands together. "My fingers... the tingling. My chest... There's something that way, in the southern field." I tear into the wheat field at full speed. She's yelling at me, but I couldn't stop if I wanted to. Something's calling my body and soul, and I'm just bearing witness. It feels so familiar, I can't explain it.

Fighting through the wheat, I finally arrive at a small muddy clearing, with a stagnant pond in the middle. "What?" I stare at it confused, searching about hoping for something else. "That's it?"

"The pond?" she says, arriving behind me, a hint of irritation in her voice. "You ran back to the pond?"

Dropping to my knees, I lean over and look at my reflection. "Can you feel it? Something's here but... This doesn't make any sense. I know this place... but I've never been here before."

"We have to go," she says, grabbing my shoulder, the irritation noticeably stronger.

"In a minute," I say, shrugging her off. I wave my hand back and forth over the pond. "Maybe it's the water? Maybe something in it?"

"We need to get to the barn," she says insistently.

Shaking my head, I reply, "Can't you feel it? It's like almost being home."

"We are going to burn to death, or be ripped apart while we burn. Let us go."

Timidly, like a child touching a celebration cake, I let one finger break the murky surface of the pond.

There's a screech in the background somewhere, but I don't care for some reason. I peek over at the oner who is standing like a statue, waiting. As much as I know we shouldn't be here, I couldn't leave even if I wanted to. My heart's pounding and my hands are trembling. I'm on the verge of bursting out with laughter or breaking down and crying. I recall feeling this way before, but I can't remember where or when.

Taking a deep breath, I plunge my arm all the way to the bottom. I fish around. "There's something here, I can feel it. I just don't know what it is..." Pulling my hand out, I stare at it. It's covered in black mud, shiny speckles here and there. "Yig!" I yelp, shaking some of it off my hand.

Sitting back on my heels, I rub my forehead, and without thinking I use the muddy hand. My eyes go wide and I jump into the pond before I know what's going on.

The oner turns to stare at me, her eyebrows up.

Laughing from the deepest part of my soul, I can't

stop slathering the mud from the shallow bottom all over my body. I roar at the sky and then look at her.

"Have you lost your mind?" she asks in that disjointed tempo of hers.

Shaking my head, I stare at my hands, turning them over and over again. "I feel more alive than I have in a long, long time. The energy... can't you feel it? The river of warm and cool running through here. It's a mana oasis... maybe all the wheat or something else protects it. It's raw and pure... there's not much, but more than I need right now." At the back of my mind, I can sense frozen memories thawing.

"You *are* a weslek," she says, taking a step back.

"Yes, so? I need my short sword."

She glares at me.

"We are on the same side. Yes, I'm a weslek." I hold my hand out. "I need my sword."

The oner just keeps staring at me.

"The scar along the chest of that carn, I did that. And *that* was when I was at half-strength and didn't know what I was capable of. Now, I think I can give us a fighting chance. But I need to do something first, it's my backup... just in case."

She lowers her gaze for a second.

Shaking my head, I gesture again with my open hand. "You already knew I was a weslek, that's why you mentioned the levi-car. I don't know how you knew, but you knew. So move on with it, give me my sword, and let's get the yig out of here."

She takes another step back, both serrated swords in her hands now.

"Woo, put those down. What are you doing?"

"The leecher could be inside you, infecting you, her own twisted version of our blessing roaming around in your mind," she says. Her face almost looks like she's fighting the words.

I put my hands up slowly. "Leechers don't work that way. She's dead, and I'm fine."

"We cannot afford that risk."

"You need me to charge and drive the levi-car, or can you drive one?"

She glances away, thinking.

I put my hand up. "Do you feel that?"

"We already—"

"Not this, not the pond. That. That deep... that haunting sound? It's more than I can feel it rather than hear it." I turn to face the west and my mind goes numb for a second. "What's wrong with the sky?"

She follows my gaze and we stare at where the blue afternoon sky changes to flaming red. She takes a step back. "That... that's the rage of the carn," she says. I'm unconvinced.

Pointing at it, I shake my head. "That looks like

gods are reigning fury down on the world, and gods don't exist."

"It's the carn," she says, turning to me. Her hands are jittering. If she's scared, then I'm terrified.

"Give me my short sword."

She stares at me again.

"Look! I have no interest in controlling a colony or harming you. I just want to get to Banareal. I need to figure out the missing parts of my past, and who killed me. More importantly, I'm not interested in dying today, are you?"

"You're a weslek, why do you need it?"

I stop myself from answering. My gaze keeps flipping between her and the fiery sky. It's like a fire storm, and I can't help but feel that it's coming our way.

The question makes me twitch. "I serve no Wizard, if that's what you're asking. I'm not part of whatever that is. I escaped a long, long time ago." There's something disconnected about her questions, and her expression. Maybe oners are terrible under pressure. "Like you, I'm my own master." I can't help but stare at the flaming sky. Neither of us has much of a chance against the carn on our own, never mind whatever that is. May I please have my short sword?"

"I told you, it's the carn."

"I don't believe you," I reply, wincing as I realize

that's not going to help me get my sword back. Surprisingly, she tosses it to me. I plunge it deep into the mud and crouch down in the murky water. Shutting my eyes tight, I concentrate on the image of a river of silver and blue light coming out of the ground, through me, and into the sword. It's peace and serenity and joy and--

"Wake up!" she yells in my face, shaking me.

Blinking repeatedly, I nod.

"Yig, that fire storm's getting closer."

She points to a plume of smoke in the west. "The carn has set the fields ablaze. We need to head to the barn before our path is cut off."

I glance at the short sword; it's glowing a healthy blue. I slip it into my belt.

"Take this," she says, handing me a bag.

"My pistol, thanks," I reply, slinging it over my shoulder and following her. My body's light and ready to move, what a wonderful difference.

The path seems endless until finally we emerge on the road. As we run down the hill towards the barn, I'm relieved to see it's got a significant amount of clearance around it from the potential flames. There's a few broken plows, and some other rusted farming equipment, around the barn. Some of it I don't recognize.

The barn's got an old metal roof, rusted and the

sides are rotting wood. It looks like it's been there for decades, now on its last legs. There are rocks and old farm machinery around it. The oner opens one side of the double door and ventures in.

Swallowing hard, I stop myself from looking back at the fields and sky. The wind's picking up, and I swear there's a horrifying screech being carried on it. I can't remember anything about carnu and fire storms, or having a screech like this, but the last thing I need to is rely on my sketchy memory of academia. Dealing with the oners has already reminded me of the limits of what I'd once learned.

Shaking off the sense of impending doom, I follow the oner. Inside the barn's filled with tools and a few hay bales that have seen better days. Occupying most of the space is something covered in strange, shiny tarps.

"Help me remove these," she commands, grabbing one part of the silvery covers. I help her get it off, and then stand there, stunned.

"This... this is an original two-seater levi-car. I remember these," I say, standing back to marvel at it. The poor thing's been ravaged by time and uncaring hands. Its paint is faded to a pale blue, its doors are missing, and there's no glass. Walking around it, I remove the tarps covering something behind it. "What the yig is this?"

"We found it like that," replies the oner. "It's like someone bolted a cart on the back of it."

I give her a sideways glance, but am drawn back to the modified, antique beauty. "It's more than that. This is amazing," I say peeking underneath. "Someone cannibalized a few other levis to make this flatbed a functional part of the levi-car. Look at this... the cloth webbing is still clean and firm, and the sapphire tubes are laid out expertly. Someone really knew what they were doing."

The oner's unmoved by my excitement. "We believe it was used to carry produce for trade, if it ever worked. That's what we want."

"Oh, I'm sure it did." I follow the webbing and tubes all the way back to the engine panel, which pops open easily. "These models..." I tap my fingers together and smile as a memory comes forward. "I worked one of these once. This engine's about twice the size than what the model came with. Someone's done this themselves. This panel's probably from a levi-car a generation or two later."

"Do you think you can charge it?" she asks, the stiltedness more pronounced than before.

"Yeah."

"Then get to work. We need that working immediately. The carn will be here shortly."

"Right." I get up close to the panel. "You're sure

this thing should be working? It's just the charge that's missing?"

"Yes."

Her certainty throws me off a bit, but we don't have time. The engine pieces remind me of the one I'd looked at a few days ago when I'd first met the carn. Instead of three discs, it has two, but these ones are a healthy silver. "The cloth webbing and tubes look great. Weird... I'd have expected the charging crystal to be visible, looks like they're behind everything. Weird design."

"The mechanic One... we had... mentioned it was efficient. He considered modifying it."

"Huh, I wish he would have. No way to know what's really behind all of this. It could be a waste of time."

"It's not, get it done," she commands, a hint of impatient irritation in her otherwise flat voice.

Scratching my cheek, I talk myself through how I think it works. Flashes of working with the Old Man on one in a barn similar to this one keep popping into my mind. "What did he say? The song... find the song." I stick my finger in my mouth to clean it, spitting out the gross remnants with extreme prejudice.

Cautiously, I touch the cloth webbing and follow it up to the first silver disc, and then the tubes from it to the second, and then, now up to my elbow, I finally feel something cool and flat. My face lights up as I hear the faint, sweet sound of the heart of the machine. "I found its song. That means there's no broken connections. The river of energy can flow around it and come back to the heart." The smile hurts it's so big. Pausing for a moment, I think of the Old Man. Insecurity makes me tap the short sword on my side. "You always said to bring your own end to the party, but we're not ending today. I'm coming to Banareal, and I'm going to find out what happened to you, Old Man." Something dawns on me. "Hey, do you have my map?"

The oner turns to me, her eyebrows up in a moment of surprise. She hesitates and then nods.

"Okay, good. I'm going to charge it. If it explodes and kills me, send my remains to Banareal, will you?"

She stares at me, a weird expression on her usually expressionless face. After several seconds she nods, and I start.

Closing my eyes and taking a long, steady breath, I imagine a river flowing from my core, through my arm, into the machine's heart. Sweat starts beading down my forehead and my breathing gets more intense. "Either this heart's resisting... or it's got ten hearts that all need to be awakened. Yig this is hard... Hey! Hey! The song's getting louder!"

I hear the barn door creak open. "Hurry, the carn's almost here. Give it everything you have." There's a weird finality to her voice, but I don't care. Her two serrated swords make a distinctive zing as they come out of their sheaths.

"GAH! I need more time!" I yell through gritted teeth. What was once a raging river inside me is quickly draining down to an annoyed stream. Maybe this is pointless. It's like I'm trying to lift a boulder.

"What's that deep hum?" she asks.

I open my eyes and turn my head about. "That's the engine. It's starting!" Shutting my eyes tight, I grunt and push harder. "Come on! Come on!" The deep hum grows and the engine starts vibrating.

The oner peeks out the barn door and then closes it. "The carn's coming up the path, there's fire everywhere. We're out of time."

I stop. "I thought you already said the carn was almost here." Glancing around at the barn, I shake my head. "Wait, something doesn't make sense. Why would it be coming here? You said it was pushing us towards here, but—"

She glares at me. "You need to get the levi-car up in the air! Focus!"

Nodding and with a deep breath, I give a final push.

Closing my eyes, I imagine pushing every last drop of energy out of me as hard as I can. The engine's hum grows until one corner of the levi-car lifts up with a clunk, then another. I hold on tight as each of the six levitation points kicks in and the levi-car and its flatbed stabilize. "Haha!" I yell, withdrawing my hand from the engine carefully. I stare at the silver discs as they start to pulse, heat now radiating from them. Carefully I close the panel and hop down to the ground. "We need to turn the levi around if we're going to have any chance of driving past the carn. And forget about trying to hit it with this, we don't have enough room to get up to speed." She stares at me, unflinching. I stare back, something's off. "Will you help me push?"

The oner nods.

"You push on the far end of the flatbed, while I push on the opposite front end. It's not going to want to move, remember, we've got to overcome that. Once it starts to move, it'll be easy, just like getting a cart out of a rut. Got it?"

It bothers me how she's standing there again, blinking at me. I can tell she's thinking. What's there to think about? Just when I'm about to ask her what's going on, she replies.

"Yes." She moves into position.

I search my shirt for a clean spot to wipe my face and give up. Planting my hands right beside the front levitation point, I dig my feet into the dirt floor. "Ready? Three, two, one, now! Grrr! Move! Move you yigging piece of… that's it… Come on!" Finally, with a metallic groan, the levi-car gives up its desire to stay still and lets us spin it around.

Laughing, I bend over and put my hands on my knees, letting the muddy sweat drip off my head and face. "Give me a minute and then we'll get going. With a bit of luck, we'll get passed the carn and outrun whatever freak storm that is."

The oner's lips are pulled tight, her brow hinting at something I can't pick up. "You seem tired. Will you be up for a fight?" she asks, giving me a sideways glance.

I wave her off. "Don't worry about me, I'm exhausted, but I always have a little extra in the tank for emergencies. I have to say though, that levi-car felt like it had ten hearts, not one. Maybe someone over-engineered it? It was like it was made to empty me out." Taking a deep breath and straightening up, I point at door. "Speaking of fights..." I look about, shaking my head, "shouldn't the carn be here by now? Not that I want to die but... what's going on?"

She stares at me, blinking. There's that eerie delay again fragmenting her reaction. Her head moving back then stopping, her mini-expression then changing, and so on.

Squinting at her, I lick my lips. "There's no carn, is there?" Scanning about, I spy my bag on the flatbed. Keeping an eye on her out of the corner of my eye, I decide to go for my short sword.

She taps the flat sides of her swords together and points them at me. "Drop your sword."

My shoulders slump and I sigh as I let it fall and put my hands up. "Randmon, you around? You should have told me I was being an idiot." I glance up at her, surprised she's not telling me to shut up.

The barn doors are thrown open, drawing my attention but not hers. A thunder of footsteps flood in as the leecher walks in, leaning on a long staff, a stream of oners behind her walking in pairs. Each of them is perfectly synchronized to her steps, until she stops a few feet in front of me. The barn falls silent, at first, then the rumble from the distant storm fills the room.

"I thought I killed you," I say to the leecher. I put

my hands down and tilt my head down too, but I keep my gaze up. Given that leechers are usually poor, desperate people, I'm hoping my posture will feed her need to feel powerful.

She's dressed in a long black dress, wrapped in an old, knitted shawl that's fraying. Her darker side looks less withered than last time, and there's no sign of any wounds from my pistol. Maybe I shot her where she's covered? Her face looks almost pained with concentration, a look echoed by the oners, except for the woman oner who's been keeping me company.

The leecher smiles at the levi-car and then turns her attention to me. "While you wounded me, you killed one of them. Close though. Now it's time for me to return the favor." Her speech is distracted, similar to the woman oner. I glance at the others, no one's moving a muscle. I can't imagine how much mana it's taking for her to control them all.

"You can't kill me, not yet. You need me to drive. Where you're going, you need to be able to outrun that fire storm." I put my hands up, again keeping my head bowed.

She sighs and thinks.

I figure back at the bar when I met her, everyone there was probably a oner, maybe special ones like the woman. But the leecher wasn't concentrating like this then... maybe something's changed or maybe she can't afford to exert full control the whole time. Peeking at the woman oner, I wonder if she'd managed to say anything to me that didn't come from the leecher. No way to know.

"I have to thank you. If you hadn't wounded me, I'd never have thought of keeping you alive and feeding off you. I would have ended you then, like I did the carnu. That was a feast on power like I've never had before. But sadly, unlike you weslek, I can't keep the mana I don't use quickly. It fades so fast. I sipped the mana from you as I got better, but you kept getting weaker. That was, until my oners told me of the mana pond. Imagine how delighted I was to learn that you could be rejuvenated without having to be conscious. All it cost me was some mana to keep you asleep while they coated you in mud, then they'd clean you up, and I'd get back ten times the mana in return. I hope you didn't mind the shave, but it was disgusting. It was a fun few months. A shame my spies spotted the—"

"Months?" I run my hand through my muddy hair. "No way." It makes sense though. I knew the wheat wasn't that tall before. I'm not even sure it was planted yet.

She laughs. "What, did you believe this One?" she says pointing at the woman. "She's a good liar, the best of the group. She's also the most stubborn of the all my oners. There's even part of the original person there, deep underneath the blessing. But despite her best, there's no fighting the blessing and me."

A shadow falls over the barn and I see panic flash on the face of the leecher. "Time to drive."

"I'm not moving until you tell me what the yig's going on."

The leecher glares at me, but she knows I'm holding at least one decent card in our game.

"That's not a fiery storm, that's the floating city of Ashleek. The storm is ripping up every ounce of mana and life force it can find. The city's set on a column of raging flame to charge itself."

"What are you talking about?"

She laughs at me. "How do you think the wasteland was made? The rim exists because magic's stronger there. They chain wesleks like you to the bottom of their cities and connect you to some monstrous machine. The entire city feeds on them and uses them, like I did you."

My heart's pounding like crazy. "What are you talking about? That's..." Words fail me. A memory flashes of seeing a machine... There was an adept there... and... the Old Man, too. I must have been trying to stop it, but it happened anyway. Who was I? "They can't do that."

"Can't? I lived in the under-city of Nashamere, it was the first. You're a weslek, you know what it's like to be part of the servant class, and what it means to be one of the rodents. People like me were the rodents, suddenly found to have a purpose, to feed the needs of the regime as fuel."

I've got to find the Old Man. We need to stop this... Wait, I remember trying. Killing... who was it? Shaking off the memory, I focus. "It looks like we're out of time. I can see the column of fire. They're pulling the life force from the fields," I say pointing at the barn door.

The woman oner head turns and she takes a step, then freezes.

The leecher's face twists and contorts. Her hands jittering as the oners twitch, small groups of them moving in synch. Right before my eyes, the leecher's face wrinkles and parts go dark, then patches start to change to ashy black, the skin looking like sun-beaten leather. She cradles an arm up against her chest as her fingers go black and the nails fall off, one by one.

Licking my lips first, I snatch my short sword and bury it deep into the leecher's chest. Knocking her backwards, I scramble to my feet and on to the flatbed of the levi-car and dive for my bag.

Chaos erupts as the oners' unified mind shatters. Some start reaching out for me, some turn to the leecher, and some run outside into the fire storm.

I pull my pistol out of my bag and slap the switch

so it's powered by my mana. As oners grab at me, I reach as deep into my core as I can to blow holes in as many of them as I can, but it's pointless. In a heartbeat, I'm pulled down, my pistol lost, and I find myself being kicked and stomped on from every angle.

Suddenly everything stops. With a single, bloody eye barely able to open, I gaze at the leecher. She's sitting beside me, being held up by a blood-soaked oner. Her face is pale; her breathing is shallow. The front of her dress is drenched in blood. She's clutching her chest with one hand, and my short sword in the other. The woman oner is standing behind her, a statue.

"Why did you ruin everything?" the leecher yells, the roar from the floating city now starting to shake the ground.

"You were going to kill me at the first chance you got... or make me your battery again. And if you think you can outrun that?" I point with my chin at the yig outside, "You're a fool." Everything inside and out goes red. We must be at the outer edge of the mana-drain. I can't even imagine the scale of what's being done. There's not much time.

I look the leecher in the eyes and growl. "I'm not dying today!" I force myself up and make a sloppy move for her. She stabs me right in the stomach with my short sword and pushes me over. The pain is horrible. My hands shake in front of me as I fight to stay conscious. Got t touch the hilt...

The leecher spits on me and screams, "Is that what you wanted? Is—" She's cut-off as two serrated blades come through her chest.

Kicking the leecher aside, the woman oner looks down at me. Her expression should have tears with it, but it doesn't.

I want to say something, but I can't. The front of the barn vanishes as the roaring flame starts taking everything around us apart. Every breath is agony, and harder than the one before it. I feel like I'm drowning.

The woman oner grabs one of the strange, shiny tarps.

I look about with my one good eye. "Randmon, are you there? I'm sorry... Forgive me... I... no other way... I'm sorry..." I mouth. Coughing up blood, I try one more time to get my hands to the hilt, to no avail.

Glancing about desperately, I catch my reflection in the blade of the short sword, and my heart skips a beat. That face... it's not mine. Old Man, is that you?

The woman throws the tarp over me and part of the levi-car and climbs underneath. She pushes me right under the body of the levi, right under the array of charging crystals, and pulls the tarp down tightly. That done, she reaches for my short sword. I use everything I've got to groan and shake my head. She nods, her eyes sorrowful.

There's no air.

I can't keep my eye open anymore. There's a soothing touch on my hands, closing them. For a moment red shines through my eye lids and I feel tremendous heat, and then... nothing. The world's gone.

The End

of

Season One

THANK YOU
FOR READING THIS BOOK

Reviews are powerful and are more than just you sharing your important voice and opinion, they are also about telling the world that people are reading the book.

Many don't realize that without enough reviews, indie authors are excluded from important newsletters and other opportunities that could otherwise help them get the word out. So, if you have the opportunity, I would greatly appreciate your review.

Don't know how to write a review? Check out **AdamDreece.com/WriteAReview**. Where could you post it? Your favorite online retailer site and GoodReads.com are a great start!

Don't miss out on sneak peeks and news, join my newsletter at: **AdamDreece.com/newsletter**

Thank you,

Adam

ABOUT THE AUTHOR

With a best-selling young adult series, The Yellow Hoods, well underway, and a successful episodic series, The Wizard Killer, I decided it was time to share my deep love of science fiction with The Man of Cloud 9. It allowed me to pull from my over 20 years of experience in software, from leading teams at a Silicon Valley startup and working on huge projects at companies like Microsoft.

Like many people, I wrote and wrote but did practically nothing with it. Maybe I would be an author *someday*. Then two medical events, one after the other, made me change my priorities. With the amazing support of my wife and kids, I kicked off a serious indie author career, and the response has been amazing.

I live in Calgary, Alberta, Canada with my awesome wife, amazing kids, and lots and lots of sticky notes and notebooks.

I blog about writing, life and more at **AdamDreece.com**. Join me on Twitter **@adamdreece**, on Facebook at **AdamDreeceAuthor** or send me an email **Adam.Dreece@ADZOPublishing.com**

PLAYLIST

Every now and then I get asked what albums I listened to when writing a book. Here's what I primarily listened to when writing The Wizard Killer - Season One:

Game of Thrones season 3 soundtrack
Game of Thrones season 5 soundtrack
by Ramin Djawadi

Metallica by Metallica

Razor's Edge by AC/DC

The Best of Southern California Punk Rock

This is War by Thirty Seconds to Mars

Enjoy,
Adam

ADAM DREECE BOOKS

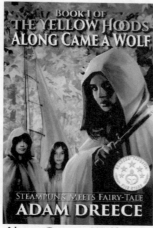

Along Came a Wolf
ISBN: 978-0-9881013-0-2

Breadcrumb Trail
ISBN: 978-0-9881013-3-3

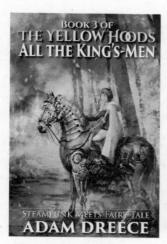

All the King's-Men
ISBN: 978-0-9881013-6-4

Beauties of the Beast
ISBN: 978-0-9948184-0-9

Watch for Book 5, coming Spring 2017